A Lion's

Pride

By

Alyssa Rae

This is a work of fiction. Names, characters, places and incidents either are the product of the author's imagination or are used fictitiously, and any resemblance to actual persons, living or dead, business establishments, events, or locales is entirely coincidental. The publisher does not have any control over and does not assume responsibility for author or third-party websites or their content.

ISBN: 978-0615761732

For my mother who supported and helped me through the whole process and for my father who let me live with them for free.

And

For my grandparents who I love very much, especially my Grandfather who owes me twenty bucks.

Prologue

Her hands were tied in front of her. The rope was tight around her wrists, rubbing the skin raw and cutting off the circulation in her hands. It was nighttime now; darkness flooded into the locked room. She retied the loose strings on her sneakers, grateful that she had been smart enough to put them on that morning and wishing that she had taken the time to put on a pair of socks too. She woke to a day that felt like a dream, but the dream had quickly faded into a nightmare.

She closed her eyes, but sleep was impossible. She tried to recall as many details as she could about where she was. The ride here wasn't long, maybe 20 minutes, which meant she couldn't be that far outside of town. She was driven here in the back of a gray, windowless van. When the van stopped, she was pulled out so fast she could barely take in her surroundings. She was able to catch glimpses of a log cabin, situated off the main road and on the outskirts of woods.

There were at least 10 men on guard at the cabin; it had taken six to bring her here: three on motorcycles, two in the van and one that didn't make it back. The man who rode in the back of the van with her tied her wrists together tightly with rope and left his gun pointed to her chest for the entire ride. When they arrived at least four more had been waiting at the cabin. Each man was heavily armed, carrying a machine gun in his hands, a 9mm holstered under his jacket, and she was willing to bet each one of them had a knife hidden somewhere on their person. Some of the men looked familiar to her, which was no surprise. Before they managed to lock her in this room, she heard one of them mention more would be coming later that day. A small army guarding a log cabin and a single twenty-something year old girl; it seemed ridiculous, but in reality it wasn't. The men knew the kind of friends that she had, and knew they would be coming for her, and fast. They had been smart to prepare.

But the men had made one crucial mistake

when bringing her here; no one had thought to search her pockets when they grabbed her. She always carried her father's pocket knife wherever she went. The knife had been in her shorts pocket when the men picked her up, right next to her cell phone which she knew her friends were tracing now or would be soon. The second the men left her in this locked room she jumped into action. One of them would realize the mistake and would come back to check her. She had to hide the knife and the phone before they did.

The room was made entirely of wood, the inside walls matching the log cabin's outside walls, with hardwood floors. The room was bare with no furniture and no place to hide. She quickly got down on all fours and crawled on the floor, testing the floorboards with the hope that one of them would be loose. As quietly as she could she ran her hands along the floorboards closest to the walls testing for weaknesses. She was running out of time. Finally she spotted a floorboard whose seam did not match the seam in the wall. Gently she tried to lift the board up, but it was nearly impossible to move with her fingers. She took out her knife and shoved it into the crack. She wiggled the knife until she was able to pop up the floor board. The board made a loud creak as she lifted it, tearing it from the original seam, and ripping it apart from the board next to it. She paused to make sure no one heard her before she did anything else. Afraid she wouldn't be able to lift the board up again without the knife, she sawed at the edge with the knife, leaving a gap big enough to fit her finger, but small enough to not be noticed. She dropped the phone and knife underneath and then fit the floor board back into place.

She sat down in the opposite corner of the room across from the door, hoping that she would be able to keep their attention away from the cracked floor board where she hid the phone and the knife. This was the best she could do for now. Moments later the door to the room opened again and one of the men from the van walked in. He grabbed her wrists and pulled her up off the floor until she was standing in front of him. The man smirked as he began to run his hands over her clothes checking all of her pockets and even inside her shirt. She had been right about hiding her phone and knife and had managed to do it just in the nick of time. The man continued to smirk even after he was finished. He stood facing her, his hands holding her tied wrists that were already bleeding from the tight rope.

"I could have protected you," he said. "You never gave me a chance."

She didn't respond, instead she stared him down, never breaking eye contact. He was a big man and she knew she had no chance of overpowering him. Even if she did manage to bring him down, there were still nine more outside the door. No, she would wait; her time for revenge would come. Her cell phone was on. Her friends would know her location in just a few hours. They would find her, *he* would find her, and then they would come for her. She only hoped they wouldn't be too late.

Chapter One

Donnie sipped his coffee out of his favorite travel mug as he waited at a red light. He was on his way home to pull an all-nighter on his latest project for his Technology class. Out of the corner of his eye, he saw a car pull up next to him at the light. He looked over at the other driver and saw one of his oldest friends from high school. The driver's windows were all the way down and Donnie could hear the radio playing at full volume. He waved to his friend who smiled back and, then he tightened his hands on the steering wheel. The driver revved the car engine in a challenge to Donnie. Donnie smiled and placed his coffee mug in the cup holder. The traffic light turned green and both drivers floored the gas pedal. The driver maneuvered in front of Donnie so he couldn't pass and then they slammed on the brakes. Donnie struggled to stop his car in time. His coffee mug flew out of the cup holder and spilled all over the car's console and Donnie's clothes. When Donnie looked up from the coffee spill, his friend's car was already through the next traffic light. A hand waved to him out of the window.

The car tires screeched as the driver made the tight turn into the parking lot at "Murphy Automotive." The car stopped only inches from the main garage door, the radio blasting the driver's favorite song: Lonely Boy by The Black Keys. Coincidentally the same song was playing on the radio in the garage. Leo, the local mechanic, stepped outside to meet the driver, followed by his new assistant, Sean. A beautiful, young woman climbed out from the old, black 1998 Nisan Maxima.

"Hey Alex," Sean called to the girl getting out of the car, "it's our song!" Alexia Murphy, known as Alex to her friends, danced her way into the garage and over to Sean who put down the tool he was using and started to dance with her. The two of them danced as badly as they knew how; arms flailing above their heads, shaking their equally short hair around, and bobbing their heads in time to the music. Sean took Alex's hand and spun her around and then dipped her low as the song wrapped up and a commercial for a new store opening came on. They finished their dance panting and laughing together. Behind them Leo cleared his throat, demanding their attention.

"Hey Leo, what's up?" Alex asked completely out of breath from dancing. Sean put her back on her feet properly and she thanked him for the dance and walked up to Leo to give him her customary peck on the check. Leo was oily and greasy from working in the shop all day, so she touched him as little as possible to avoid getting her clothes dirty.

"Not too much. We've been pretty busy today." Leo replied. "The kid's driving me crazy," Leo tilted his head in the direction of Sean, whom had only been working for him a couple of weeks. Sean wasn't exactly a kid; he was two years older than Alex. They had gone to high school together, and had spent a lot of time together with some of their other friends. He left after graduating high school and moved into the city with his twin sister, Elise. He stayed there for a little over a year, but had gotten himself into some kind of trouble and decided to

3

come back home. His sister had met a guy and got married; now they were traveling the world.

"He can't be that bad," Alex said. Sean was a nice guy who desperately wanted to become a member of the Fu Lions Motorcycle Club, which co-owned this auto shop. He was currently on a trial basis, working in the garage and doing small favors for the club until they would decide whether to let him become a member.

"You have no idea," Leo replied shaking his head.

"How's your sister, Seany?" Alex called out to him.

"Elise? She's doin' pretty good. I think she's in Paris right now. So what brings you by today?"

"Actually I was going to ask if you guys could take a look at my car. It's been making that weird noise again and the brake light came on yesterday."

"Sure, I'll take a look at it," Leo said. "I might not be able to get to it 'til tomorrow morning."

"That's alright; I can get someone to give me a ride to class tomorrow. I need to tell Uncle Ronnie that I'm leaving it here though. Where is he?"

"He's up at the clubhouse, in his office."

"Thanks Leo, I'll see you later." Alex headed out of Murphy Automotive and made her way across the parking lot toward the clubhouse.

"Bye, Alex," she turned and waved to Sean, who had stepped outside the garage door to say goodbye to her. He gave another little shake of his hair, a signature dance move of his, and she responded by wiggling her hips back in forth, then kicked her leg up and flung her head back as she turned to walk away.

"Sean where are you? Get back in here I need your help!" Leo yelled from inside the garage. Alex laughed as she continued to the clubhouse. She could still hear Leo yelling when she reached the clubhouse door across the parking lot.

The clubhouse was situated on the other side of the parking lot, across from the auto shop. Murphy Automotive was built a couple of years after the Lions built their clubhouse. At first, the clubhouse was a meeting place for the Lions to discuss motorcycles, club business, and guy stuff, but eventually the Lions opened the bar up to the public and allowed anyone from town or visiting nearby to come in and have a drink. The bar provided extra revenue for the club and its members.

Alex stepped inside of the clubhouse and nodded to Dennis, a long time member of the club, who was standing behind the bar getting it ready to open in a couple of hours. She made her way down the long back hallway that led to the President's office, passing the three furnished bedrooms that were there for the use of any of the members who might need to spend the night. At the end of the hallway, a motorcycle was sitting on display in a little alcove built into the wall. Alex walked up to it. The motorcycle had belonged to her grandfather and had been handed down to her father. Alex's great-grandfather was the original founder of the club and his bike had been on display here for many years, but after Alex's own father was killed the club voted to replace the old bike with her father's. Pictures of her great-grandfather, grandfather, father, and uncle all hung on the wall behind the bike; all four of them were dead now. The display had been set up in their honor.

Alex stepped up onto the display platform, and checking to make sure no one was going to walk down the hallway, she threw her leg over the bike and sat down.

"Hey Dad," she whispered to the motorcycle. She knew he couldn't hear her, but being on this bike was when she felt the closest to him. It was when she was able to remember him the most. The motorcycle was a 1950s Harley Davidson Panhead, an antique, painted a dark, glossy, blue with the head of a lion detailing the front. The kickstand, which held the bike up in the alcove, was the shape of a lion's paw, and the back of the bike ended in the shape of a lion's tail. Leo was in charge of the bike's upkeep which was very simple on this kind of motorcycle. It was also a softail bike which meant that there were shocks under the seat that would absorb the worst of the bumps on the road, making for a smooth and comfortable ride. She closed her eyes and rested there for a few minutes; her hands on the handlebars and her feet on the pedals balancing the bike on its wheels. She knew how to ride, but driving a car was much more practical for her day-to-day life, especially since she was raising her little sister on her own.

Reluctantly she opened her eyes and climbed down from the bike. To the right of the display was a staircase leading up to an apartment on top of the clubhouse. Her childhood friend Jason, the Vice President of the club and the son of the current President, was living there now. She contemplated going up to say hello to him, but instead she turned left and walked into the President's office.

"Hey Alex, I wasn't expecting you today," Ron greeted her.

"Hey Uncle Ronnie, how's it going?"

"Pretty good, what can I do for you?"

"I came by to tell you that I'm leaving the Maxima with Leo. It's been making that weird noise again. I thought I'd come say hi since I was here."

"Are you teaching tonight?"

"No, I have the night off. I was on my way home." Alex had just recently opened a music studio, where she was teaching piano lessons to young kids from town. She had been open for 6 months now and was teaching 25 lessons a week. She decided to go back to school to get a degree in music education and was attending classes twice a week at the local Community College down the road.

"Need a ride home?" Ron asked her

"No, I can walk, it's not that far."

"Absolutely not! Jason will give you a ride to classes tomorrow and he can take you home now too. Right Jason?"

"Sure," Alex hadn't even heard Jason come in. She turned to find him standing in the doorway right behind her.

"It's fine, really, I don't need a ride," Alex protested.

"Alex don't be ridiculous, you're not taking the bus. What time are your classes tomorrow?" Ron left no room for argument.

"Come on, Alex, I don't mind," Jason said.

"Alright. Pick me up at 8:30; my class is at 9:00. I'll see you later, Uncle Ronnie," Alex turned to leave.

"Hey, aren't you forgetting something?" Ron smiled and presented his cheek to her tapping it with one of his fingers. Alex crossed the office and stepped around Ron's desk to plant a kiss on his cheek. "That's more like it. Now get out of here."

"Bye Uncle." Alex and Jason left the office together. Alex was not actually related to Ron, but their families had always been very close. Her father and real uncle had grown up in town with Ron and had been best friends with him their whole lives. The three of them had been inseparable as teenagers and even more so as adults, causing trouble everywhere they went. Alex and her younger sister had spent most of their lives at Ron's house with his wife, Sara, and their son, Jason. "Uncle" was the term of endearment that Alex had given to all the members of the club. After the girls' parents and uncle died, the club stepped in and helped raise her and her sister. Sara and Ron also always made sure the girls were taken care of.

"Hey Jason, I forgot I have groceries in my car," Alex called ahead to Jason. They walked together back towards Murphy Automotive where she left her car and where Jason had parked his. She popped open the trunk of the Maxima and started to unload the groceries into Jason's car. Sean saw them and left the garage to help her carry the bags of food over to Jason's car. "Thanks Sean, but I think you need to get back. Leo's going to kill you." Alex spoke too late, Leo had already noticed Sean was missing, and he was on his way out of the garage.

"Sean, you're kidding me right?" Leo yelled from the doorway. "I was lying under a car, asking you to hand me something and no one was there. Get your butt back in here and help me! Alex you need to go home, you're too much of a distraction for my weak-minded assistant," Leo waved, and Sean slumped his shoulders as he followed him back into the garage.

"He's right you know," Jason said over the roof of his car. "You are a distraction."

"How so?"

"Whenever you come around all the guys drop what they're doing to talk to you. It's not easy to get things done when no one is paying attention or actually working."

"Oh, give me a break."

Alex rolled her eyes and got into Jason's car. The house she lived in was only about a two minutes drive away from the clubhouse. The house had belonged to the girls' parents and after they died their Uncle Jimmy, their real uncle, moved into the house with them. Their Uncle Jimmy passed away only two years ago when Alex had turned 19. Legally she was an adult and completely responsible for herself and her younger sister. The club bought the house from the bank so that the girls could continue living there and somehow ever since then Alex had figured out a way to keep her and her sister alive and comfortable. Jason pulled into the short driveway in front of the girls' small, pale yellow house with blue shutters. Together they emptied the trunk of the groceries and brought them inside.

"You can put the bags on the counter in the kitchen," she told him as he walked in behind her. When they finished unloading the car, she turned to him and said, "Thanks for the ride Jason."

"I heard you tell Dad you were going to walk home. What were you going to do about the groceries?" He had her there; he was looking at her with a raised eyebrow and that cocky smile he always got when he knew he was right.

"I hadn't thought it through, I guess." They looked at each other for a minute, and then they both burst out laughing.

Alex began emptying the bags and putting the groceries away. Jason left the kitchen and took a walk around the house. The house was small, but it was perfect for Alex and her sister, Jesse. The girls had grown up in this house and their Uncle Jimmy had lived there with them for three years after their parents' death. Jimmy Murphy died from a heart attack at the young age of 36. It had been unexpected and left everyone in shock. Alex did her best to take care of Jesse and the house, rarely asking the club for help. Money was not an issue for the girls because technically the bar and Murphy Automotive belonged to them. The businesses were owned by her family and Ron had always been a partner. The club also allowed Alex to help out from time to time. This allowed her to make extra money which she had saved up over the years. She had been working for the club long before her father was killed. They let her clean and serve food in the bar and when she was not working there, she would help out in the Auto shop. The two girls were able to live quite comfortably between the money from the business and the odd jobs Alex was doing for the club, which is why Alex finally took the risk of opening her own music studio. The club helped her find a small space to rent where she could teach and Ron helped her with the business end of things like advertising.

Alex constantly kept the house clean; everything had its place and was in order. Jason was standing in her small living room, looking at the pictures that she had hanging on the walls. There were all sorts of photos of Alex and Jesse and their family from a long time ago. A few pictures of the girls' uncle from the time they lived together hung beside the pictures of their father. There were several pictures of all the club members from cookouts and parties that had taken place over the years. Jason and his parents were in a lot of these pictures. There was even a picture of the girls' mother, the only picture they had left of her. His personal favorite was the picture that was in the center of the wall, next to their mother's photo. It was a picture of Jason, his parents, Alex, Jesse and their father at the beach. They had all spent the day on the beach together when Jason was 16, Alex was 14, and Jesse was only 6. Jason had spent the day teaching Alex how to surf, and she had just stood up for the first time, when Alex's uncle snapped the photo. Alex and Jason were standing on their surfboards side by side as they rode a wave. Jason was on the pink board and Alex was on the blue board because she refused to use the "girl board." In the corner of the picture Jason's parents were holding hands, while they watched Jesse fly a kite with her father. That was one of the best days they had all spent together; it was also one of their last. Only a month later, the girls' father was killed in a bar fight in the next town over. This was one of the last times Jason could remember when Alex was truly happy. Jesse was younger and was able to bounce back quicker, but Alex had a much harder time with things. The smile on Alex's face in this photo was the last time Jason could really remember her smiling like that. She still smiled at people, but it wasn't the same as it used to be.

"I love that picture." She startled him. She had managed to sneak up on him and was standing right beside him, their shoulders almost touching.

"That was a great day," he looked at her. She was smiling as though she was remembering something and then just as suddenly as it appeared, the smile vanished. Worried that she was remembering something bad, Jason changed the subject.

"Hey, do you need any help for the cookout this weekend?"

She came out of her day dream, shaking her

head, "No, I've got it covered. Sara's coming over, and so are some of the other wives, to help me set up. Uncle Ronnie's going to grill some hot dogs and hamburgers." Alex was hosting a cookout at the house for the first time since her uncle died. There used to be cookouts once a month at her house, but after Jimmy died, it had been too hard for her to handle everything. Her life was finally beginning to move smoothly and she decided it was time to begin the tradition again.

"Do you need me to bring anything?"

"Just the rest of my groceries from your car," she gave him a sly sideways smile and looked up at him from the corner of her eye. Jason had completely forgotten about the other grocery bags still sitting in the trunk of his car. He went back outside and finished bringing in the rest of the bags.

"Well, if that's everything then I'm gonna head out."

"Alright, Jason, I'll see you later. Don't forget to pick me up tomorrow morning."

"10:00, right?" He laughed. He knew her

classes started at 9:00.

"Very funny. You need to be here at 8:30 so I won't be late."

"Yeah, yeah I know. I'll be here." He left the house and walked out to his car.

Alex went back to putting the food away. Jason better be here tomorrow, she thought to herself; she couldn't afford to be late to class again. Thinking about class and school made Alex realize she had forgotten something.

"Crap," she said out loud and dropped the item in her hand back onto the counter and ran back outside as Jason began to back out of the driveway. "Wait!" she yelled running down the driveway waving her arms to get his attention.

He saw her and yelled, "What is it?" out of his car window.

She caught up to him at the end of the driveway, "I forgot Jess is going to need a ride home tonight from camp."

"I'll get Mom to pick her up. I've got something to do for the club later tonight." Alex knew what that meant: the club had business to handle in town, dangerous business.

"Be careful," she told him.

"I'm always careful," he responded, but when he saw the cynical look on her face he added, "Don't worry Al, I'll be fine. I'll see you in the morning," he pulled out of the driveway and headed back to the garage.

The local diner was busy that night, every table was filled and the waitresses were working hard to keep up with the orders. A man riding a bright, yellow, Harley Davidson XLH Sportster 1200 pulled into the busy parking lot and parked off to the side. He got off the motorcycle and removed his helmet. He was a young man with shaggy blonde hair and light green eyes. Anyone who quickly glanced his way would immediately avert their eyes. From the way he was dressed and the way he was acting he looked like he was a drug addict, a rarity in this town, desperate for a fix. He'd heard a rumor that there was someone selling drugs behind the diner and was here to check it out. He made sure no one was watching him and then he ducked around the corner behind the diner. There was a dark figure dressed in black, sitting in the shadows on the back steps into the restaurant. The blonde nodded to him.

"What do you want?" The dark one asked.

"I heard I could score some drugs back here. You know who's selling"?"

"What's it to ya?"

"Come on, man. I gotta know."

"You must be desperate. Not many people in this town are brave enough to buy drugs," the figure on the steps stood up and walked closer to the blonde. The blonde looked him over and discovered that the dark figure was really just a young kid, only about 17, and not very tall. He had dark black hair and piercing blue eyes.

"Aren't you a little young to be selling drugs?" The blonde asked.

"You're not in a position to be picky," the dark haired boy took a small pouch filled with a white substance from his pocket and held it up. The blonde took a roll of money out of his inner jacket pocket and tossed it to him. The boy threw the pouch over to the blonde who caught it and opened it. He took a small amount on the tip of his finger and tasted it.

"This is good stuff," the blonde said.

"I only sell the best. That's what keeps 'em comin'."

"Where'd you get it?"

"None of your business, now get outta here, I've got other business to attend to."

The dark haired boy turned his back to the blonde: a big mistake. The blonde pulled a gun out of the waistband of his jeans and placed against the back of the boy's head.

"I said, where'd you get it? Where are the Reapers getting their supply from."

"What? How did you know I was selling for the Reapers."

The blonde took a step back so the boy could turn to face him, "I didn't know, you just told me. Why'd they send a kid out here alone to do their dirty work?"

"That's where you're mistaken. I'm not alone." A confused look passed over the blonde's face. He heard a gun cock behind him, the cool feel of metal on the back of his neck.

"Reapers never work alone," said the man with the gun pointed to the blonde's head.

"That's funny, neither do Lions," the blonde said smirking.

"What?" Another gun was cocked and placed against the Reaper's neck. The blonde stepped away and took hold of the black haired boy again.

"It's about time Jason," the blonde said, "What took you so long?"

"What are you talking about, Seany? I couldn't come in until we knew who they were."

"You couldn't come in while the guy had a gun to my head?"

"Are you blind? I'm here now, aren't I?"

"Who are you people?" The Reaper asked.

"Fu Lions," Jason said. Realization hit the Reaper as Jason knocked him out, slamming the gun against his head.

"Was that necessary?" Sean asked pushing a lock of blonde hair out of his eye.

"We have to send them a message, Seany."

"Then give them a message. You don't have to beat the guy up."

"Trust me, the bump on the back of this guy's head will be message enough. You're gonna have to grow thicker skin if you want to be in this club."

"I'm just saying we're supposed to be protecting people and you going around hitting guys on the head and knocking them out, sends a mixed message, don't you think?"

"Sean, can we discuss this later, maybe not in front of our enemy."

"Fine."

Jason rolled his eyes and looked at the boy, "What's your name kid?"

"Mike."

"Mike, you're too young for this world. Go home and stay as far away from the Reapers as you can. But first, tell them the next time any of them come into our town selling drugs, they won't be leaving."

Jason and Sean left Mike and the Reaper where they were and got on their motorcycles. As they climbed onto their motorcycles, Jason saw his friend Donnie leaving the diner and walking across the parking lot to his car. Donnie was standing next to a large puddle as he waited for a car to pull out of its parking spot. Jason laughed to himself as he sped through the puddle causing it to splash and soak Donnie.

"Oh, come on man!" Donnie yelled as he tried to ring out some of the water from his shirt.

Jason and Sean waved and pulled out of the diner parking lot.

Chapter 2

The Fu Lions: ancient Chinese mythical creature believed to have special protective powers. Two of these lions would be placed outside of important buildings in an attempt to ward off evil spirits trying to get inside. They were guardians. That is how Alex's great-grandfather, Killian Murphy, chose the name of his motorcycle club. His club would protect the town he lived in against any form of evil trying to get in. Evils in the form of drugs and weapons were driven through this small town; the first stop in a long line of coastal towns

The Reaper's Sons was the name of the motorcycle club in the next town over. It was because of them that Killian and a group of men from his town decided to get together and form the Fu Lions. The Reaper's Sons were ruthless men. They dealt drugs and sold guns to the people of Killian's town. Killian got tired of watching the news and seeing the amount of people who were being unnecessarily killed with illegal weapons or from taking drugs. Two weeks later he found enough men from town who felt the same way and The Fu Lions were born. One month later they built a clubhouse where they could meet and discuss plans on how to rid their town of the Reaper's Sons. Naturally, as the founder of the club, the men thought it best to have a vote for who would lead them and decided the Presidency should go to Killian. Years later when Killian grew too old to lead, the members voted for his son to be the next President. Ever since then the Murphy's had always been chosen as the leaders. It only took two years for the Lions to chase the Reaper's out of their town and ever since the Lions have fought to keep them out.

Alex heard a scream. She threw the bed sheets off of her and ran into the living room. Two large men dressed in black were standing in the middle of the room; one of them was holding a gun to a blonde woman's head as she kneeled in front of him on the floor. The other man in black was holding another person down on the floor. Alex was confused; she looked down at herself and saw that she was wearing a long, Scooby-Doo t-shirt, her pajamas when she was 10 years old. She studied the scene closer and realized that it was her father being pinned to the floor underneath the man in black. He was yelling something at the man holding the gun, until he noticed Alex watching. He yelled at her to run, to get out of the room away from the men, but Alex was frozen in her place. The woman kneeling on the floor turned her head to face Alex. Alex gasped as the woman's face became her mother's. Her mother didn't say anything; instead she smiled at Alex as if to say "Everything will be okay." The gun went off and Alex's mother fell forward onto the floor. The man in black laughed as he loomed over her mother's body. Tears filled Alex's eyes and poured over onto her cheeks. She stared straight into the shooter's face, but there was nothing there; the tears blurred her vision.

Alex woke panting with tears streaming down her cheeks. She rolled over and peered at her alarm clock with groggy eyes. The clock said it was 6:30, time to get up and ready for the day. Instead she lay there remembering the night her mother was killed. The dream was always the same, an exact replica of that horrible night. She saw the man's face that night, but her mind forced her to forget. She did however remember his voice. His voice was deep and gravelly with an evil twinge on the edge of it. She remembered how he laughed as he left the house, a sinister laugh that every bad character in movies had.

She turned her mind over to more positive thoughts. She began to think about the history of the Fu Lions that her father told her when she was young. Most little girls got fairy tale stories when they went to bed, but not Alex, she got stories about the Fu Lions; stories about how the club came to be and how they were able to drive the Reaper's Sons away.

Alex looked at the clock again and then covered her head with the pillow. She knew she had to get up, but she just didn't want to; Thursdays were her longest day of the week. Ron's wife, Sara, would be at the house to pick Jesse up at 8:00, and then Jason was supposed to be there by 8:30. Slowly, Alex crawled out of the bed and made her way into the bathroom. The bathroom was very small with only a shower and no tub, a small sink and countertop, and a toilet, but there was only the two of them. Recently the girls re-decorated the bathroom with an "Under the Sea" theme. They painted the walls a light blue, and bought fished-shaped rugs and soap dishes. There was a green shower curtain facing out and a plastic surfboard curtain facing the inside, held up by fish shaped curtain holders that matched the rugs.

Alex caught a glimpse herself in the mirror as she walked into the bathroom. Her eyes stopped on the chain around her neck. Her necklace was a simple silver chain that held a pendant given to her when she was born. The pendant was the shape of a Lion of Fu's head with fierce, rubies for eyes. She and her sister both wore the same necklace and neither of them had ever taken it off.

She thought she looked worn out and tired, not only because she was unable to sleep well the night before, but because of the toll the last four years had taken on her. The girls' mother was murdered when Alex was 10 and Jesse was 3. A break-in that had gone completely wrong, at least that's the story she'd been told. In reality they also lost a piece of their father that night. He was never the same again and sometimes he would cry himself to sleep when he thought the girls couldn't hear him. He swore an oath on his wife's grave that he wouldn't rest until he found the man who did this and kill him.

Although he was torn with grief he did his best to raise his girls on his own, with occasional help from the club. Every morning he would take the girls to school and then go to work in the auto garage he, and his brother, Jimmy, owned. "Murphy Automotive," was built in the same parking lot as the Fu Lions clubhouse the year the club had been founded, and was owned by the Murphy's. In the afternoons the school bus would drop Alex off at the garage, where she spent hours doing her homework while watching her father and uncle work on the cars. Both of the girls enjoyed spending time in the garage and at the clubhouse. Kevin Murphy loved his daughters; they were the only thing that kept him going after his wife's death. That and his promise for revenge. Even so, Alex had always felt bad that her father never had a son that could follow in his footsteps and become the next President of the club.

One night, as her father was helping Jesse change into her pajamas for bedtime, Alex asked him if he would have rather had a son. In reply he said, "I wouldn't trade you two girls for a hundred sons."

"But Dad, who are you going to teach mechanic and car stuff to? And who'll be the next President of the club, if you don't have a son?"

Kevin thought for a moment before he answered, "My brother, Jimmy could be president or maybe one of the other guys like Russell or Ronnie. I don't need a son to take over the club, Alex, any of the other guys could do it."

"Then who are you gonna teach all your guy stuff to? Like being a mechanic? I'm not very good at it."

"Nonsense! You're a great little helper in the garage. Leo loves having you around, besides I've always got Jesse here. Who knows? Jesse might become a great mechanic one day." He finished putting on her pajamas and tickled Jesse's little tummy, which was received with a fit of giggles from both girls.

A giggling Alex said, "There's no such thing as a girl mechanic, daddy."

"Of course there is. Alex, you and your sister can be whatever you want to be."

"Even a member of the Lions?" Alex asked with her most serious face.

"A girl has never been voted in before, but it's not impossible."

"Do you think the club would ever vote me in?"

"I think that there may come a time when the club will need a woman to lead them. A woman that will be able to show them the way, but it will take a certain woman, a special woman, to be able to do that."

"Could I be that woman?"

"Maybe one day, why not? Enough now, it's time for you to go to bed." Kevin Murphy, Jr. tucked his daughter into bed that night, the same way he did every night, and told her tales about the Fu Lions until she fell asleep. Before he left her room he whispered, "I think that you'll grow up to be the only woman strong enough to lead the Lions." He kissed her forehead, shut the lights off, and left her bedroom.

Alex smiled at the memory. Her father didn't know it then, but she had been awake when he whispered to her. She never forgot what he said and had been determined ever since that moment to become the first female member of the Fu Lions Motorcycle Club. She turned the shower water on and waited until the bathroom filled with steam that covered the mirror before she got in. She dreaded these long moments when there was no one around and she was left alone with her thoughts. Her mind would wander back to the memories of her family when they were still together, still alive and happy. The memories from before her parents' deaths would come back at these moments to haunt her. Alex had a great life until the year she turned 10 and her mother was murdered in front of her. After that her father did his best, but it could never be the same, and when she turned 16 her father was also killed.

Kevin Murphy, his brother Jimmy, Ron and Kip, another club member and close friend, all rode their bikes out of town for a night of fun. The four of them rode to a bar in one of the small, nearby towns for a "Boy's Night Out." Sara invited Alex and Jesse to her house for dinner, so they wouldn't have to be home alone all night. Jason made them popcorn after dinner and the three of them watched a movie together in the living room. Sara went back to her room to read for a little while and after the movie the three kids decided to play cards.

Jesse was beating both Alex and Jason at the card game, making Alex laugh and Jason angry. Jason was one year older than Alex. They were all having a great time, until 10:30 p.m. when Ron called the house. The phone rang in the middle of their fourth game of Rummy and Sara came out of her bedroom to get the phone.

"Hello," she answered. "Oh, hey hon. Yea

the girls are here. I didn't have the heart to take them back to an empty house yet. What? What's wrong? Oh my god." Alex and Jason looked up at the same time. Sara's bright beaming smile was replaced by a look of sheer horror as she listened to Ron speak. A knot developed n the pit of Alex's stomach and she knew at that second that something had gone horribly wrong. Sara ran out of the living room with the phone. Alex and Jason looked at each other, and then at Jesse who didn't seem to have noticed what happened.

"Hey Jess, my mom made cookies, why don't you go have one."

"Good idea Jason. I think you could use a break from cards anyway," Jess jumped up and went into the kitchen.

Alex waited for her to be out of listening range, then turned to Jason and asked, "What are you thinking?"

"The same thing you are. This is not good."

"What do we do?"

Let's wait for mom to come back."

They waited, distracting Jesse as best as they could until Sara finally came out of her bedroom. Sara's face said it all; her eyes swollen and red from crying. She looked at all three of them and finally spoke.

"Kids," she said struggling for the words. "We have to go to the hospital. There's been an accident."

"Mom, what happened?" Jason asked, but Alex already knew; she could feel it.

"Alex, Jason, come into the kitchen for a minute. Jess, why don't you watch some T.V. while I talk to them." The three of them did as they were told; Alex and Jason followed Sara to the kitchen and Jesse turned the television on.

"Alex," Sara began when they were as far away from Jesse as they could be. "As you know, the guys went to a bar tonight to hang out. Apparently when they got to the bar a group of Reapers were already hanging out there. A fight broke out. The Reapers' Vice President was there and he attacked your father. You're Uncle Jimmy jumped in and pulled your father away, but one of the other Reapers shot Jimmy. Kip and Ron managed to drag Jimmy and Kevin out of the bar, but the Reapers got away. The guys are at the hospital now. Jimmy was shot in the shoulder and is going to be fine."

"And my father?"

"Your father, he was...he was shot as well. The bullet went into his stomach. The ambulance came and took him away to the hospital and he was still alive when they reached the hospital, but there were complications...I'm so sorry Alex, the damage was just too much. He died in the hospital." Sara couldn't look at Alex as she said it, she wanted to be strong for Alex, and she knew if she looked at Alex's face she would lose it.

"No! It's not true! It can't be!" Alex looked to Jason, tears streaming down her face. Jason would never forget that look. He wrapped his arms around Alex, but she fought him off. She hit and punched him, but he refused to let go. Eventually all of the fight went out of her and she allowed him to hold her while she cried. Jason held her weeping body in his arms until she was able to regain control over herself.

"Everyone else?" Jason asked his mother over Alex's shoulder.

"Kip broke some ribs in the fight. They're all banged up a little, but they're going to be fine."

"How am I gonna tell Jess?" Alex sobbed. "I can't do it, Sara please." Sara was heartbroken; it had been hard enough telling Alex, she hadn't even thought about telling Jesse.

"I'll do it," Jason said. He left the kitchen and went into the living room to tell Jesse. Telling Jesse the only parent she had ever known was now gone was one of the hardest things Jason ever had to do. Jesse was only 7.

After he told her, Jesse ran into the kitchen and into her sister's arms. Alex kneeled down and embraced her younger sister. They stayed wrapped in each other's arms for a long time before Alex stood up, wiped her face, and nodded to Sara.

"I'm ready," she said. "We need to get to the hospital."

They drove in silence, apart from the

occasional sob from Jesse. Alex sat in the back seat, Jesse still clinging to her older sister. The hospital wasn't far away, but the ride seemed to stretch on and on. When they finally arrived, Sara led the way to the section Ron said they would wait for them. In the elevator Jason made eye contact with Alex for the first time since they left the kitchen. He looked away from her quickly, but Alex could still see that there were tears in his eyes. The two families had spent so much time together that Alex sometimes forgot that they weren't really related.

Ron was waiting for them when the elevator doors opened. He embraced his wife and whispered something in her ear; Alex never found out what he said.

"Where's my uncle?" Alex asked Ron.

"He'll be back in a couple minutes, he had to fill out some paperwork," Alex could see the lie written all over Ron's face. "He told me to keep you girls here until he came back. Let's go see Kip; he's in a room just down the hall on the right."

"Sara, can you take my sister to see Kip? I

want to ask Uncle Ronnie something."

"Sure, come on Jess." Alex released her sister to Sara, and then turned back to Ron.

"Where is my Uncle?" She asked.

"I told you already, he's…"

"No, I've known you my whole life and I can tell when you're lying. Where is he really?" Ron promised Jimmy that he wouldn't tell her, but he knew that if he lied to her again she would just figure it out on her own anyway. It would be better to just tell her the truth now, before she tried to make a scene.

"He's in the Morgue…with your father. They're in the basement."

Alex walked away from Ron and pushed the button for the elevators.

"Wait, Alex," Ron yelled after her. "I promised Jim I'd keep you up here" Alex ignored him and stepped onto the elevator.

"I'll go with her Dad," Jason said. He had to run to catch the elevator. He shoved his arm between the doors before they could close.

"Don't try to stop me, Jason," Alex said to him.

"Wouldn't dream of it."

The doors closed and Ron was left standing in the hallway, watching the floor numbers go down. They stopped on the

letter B.

The basement was three floors down from Kip's hospital room. Leading the way Alex followed the signs down the winding hallways to the Morgue. They had to walk down a long hallway, turn right, and then turn left before they reached the clearly labeled door that said, "Morgue." Alex and Jason stopped before they turned the last corner and peered around the wall where there was a clear view of the Morgue door. There was only one door in and out of the Morgue and it was protected by a security lock. The lock would only open if a doctor's security badge with the proper codes was swiped through a badge reader. A young doctor in a lab coat was standing in front of the door reading paperwork on a clipboard, his name badge clipped to his jacket pocket in plain sight.

"What's the plan, Al?" Jason asked.

"I need to see my father," Alex whispered over her shoulder. I'm going to take that doctor's badge. After I get it, you distract him so I can get inside."

"Fine. Are you sure you want to do this?"

"Just do it, Jason."

Alex left him at the end of the hallway and made her way towards the doctor. She made it look like she was going to walk past him, but pretending to not pay attention she purposefully bumped into the doctor. Her hand brushed over his lab coat pocket and unclipped his name badge as her body slammed against his. In one fluid motion she had taken his badge and slid it into her own jeans pocket. The doctor was very young and she felt bad because she knew this would get him into trouble later, but it was too late to worry about that.

"Oh! Excuse me, I'm so sorry. I wasn't paying any attention." Alex put on her best smile and batted her eyelashes at the young doctor.

"That's ok Ms. Don't worry about it," he smiled at her. She smiled back and continued down the hallway, the doctor's badge in her pocket. She walked until she heard Jason's voice start a conversation with the doctor.

"Hey man, what's up?" She heard Jason say.

"Um, I'm sorry, can I help you?" The doctor asked looking around unsure if Jason was speaking to him or not.

"Yeah, I'm actually working on a project for school and I was wondering if I could ask you a couple of questions."

"Uh, sure. Let's make this quick though." Alex rolled her eyes, Jason did not look like the kind of kid that did his homework, and she was surprised that the doctor bought his story. The doctor was busy answering Jason's made-up questions, while Alex swiped his badge through the card reader and snuck through the door.

Immediately the temperature dropped as Alex walked through the door, but it was not the cool air that sent a chill down Alex's spine. The room was small, with two desks in the back corner and four tables spread out evenly in the center of the room. Three of the tables had very large, human sized lumps covered with white sheets. Alex was trying not to think of the "lumps" as bodies as she made her way further into the room. Each table had a clipboard hanging on a hook attached to the end. She unhooked the clipboard from the first table. The clipboard held various documents about the "lump" on the table, but Alex was only interested in the name. This particular "lump" was a middle aged woman named Deborah Smith. Alex moved on to the next clipboard, which said "Peter Murray," a man in his early forties, not her father; Alex moved on.

The third name, on the third clipboard for the third "lump" clearly read "Kevin Murphy, Jr." This name, this "lump" was her father. She walked around the table until she saw the end of the sheet. Hesitating, she thought, "Do I really want to see my father like this?" She knew the answer, no matter what she found under the sheet, was yes. Slowly she lifted the sheet.

Alex stopped herself from remembering any more. The shower water was scorching hot and felt good as it ran down her back. She washed her hair as she let the steam soak into her pores. Despite the darkness of her memory, she was able to find two things to smile about. The first was Jason. He helped her rob and distract a doctor, while she snuck into the hospital Morgue. He definitely was her best friend, because she couldn't think of anyone else who would have done that for her. The two of them had gotten into trouble together on a daily basis ever since they were small children. In fact, they still found themselves getting into trouble even though they were much older and the trouble was completely different.

The second thing that made Alex smile as she remembered that day was her Uncle Jimmy. She didn't notice him standing in the corner when she had entered the Morgue. He had watched her enter and read the label on each table until she found her father. He cleared his throat, which made her jump, before she was able to lift the sheet on her father all the way off.

"You shouldn't be in here," he said. Alex jumped and turned around.

"Where did you come from?"

"I've been in here for a while."

"What were you doing?"

"I was trying to work up the courage to do the same thing you came in here for. I haven't been able to yet."

"I had to see him, Uncle Jimmy."

"I know." He stood beside her and placed a hand on her shoulder. "We'll do it together." Jimmy lifted the sheet off his brother's body. Alex recognized her father, but she knew it wasn't him anymore; her father, the man who watched his wife get murdered and raised his two daughters by himself, the man who had tucked her into bed every night and told her stories and took her to school every day, was gone.

"What happens now, Uncle?"

"You don't need to worry about anything,

Alex, the club is going to take care of everything for us. They are already making the funeral arrangements."

"But where will we live?"

"I was thinking maybe I would move into the house with you. I'm your only living relative so the courts will be giving me custody. My house is too small, so I'll move in with you. It will be easier for Jess that way. We will make this work, Alex. I promise you, we will make this work." He put his arm around her shoulders and squeezed. While still holding his crying niece, Jim Murphy covered his dead brother's body with the white sheet. That was the last time either of them ever saw Kevin Murphy, Jr.

The reason this part of the memory made Alex smile was because of how devoted her Uncle was to taking care of his two nieces. He took good care of the girls for over three years, moving into their house and picking up where their father left off, taking his place without replacing him. Those three years they all lived together, had they not been blackened by the death of the girls' father, would have been the best three years of all of their lives. Jimmy dropped the girls off at school, made their lunches, picked Alex up from the principal's office when she got into trouble, which was more frequent after her father's death, and kissed them goodnight the same way his brother had. He loved his nieces like his own children and they loved him back. Jimmy Murphy, however, was a lot older than his brother and had a series of heart problems, which had kept him from becoming the Lion's president originally. With the death of his brother, Jimmy was voted in as the new President, taking on all of the responsibilities his brother had left behind. The burden was too much and the year Alex turned 19, Jimmy Murphy suffered from a severe heart attack.

This time Alex did not need to sneak into the hospital Morgue; her uncle died holding her hand in his hospital room. He had sent Jesse out of the room, knowing he didn't have much time left. He didn't want Jesse to watch him die, but he knew that Alex was strong and he needed her there with him.

"Come here, Alex," He motioned to the chair beside his bed.

She did as he asked, "I'm here Uncle Jimmy."

"I've made Ron a partner in the garage. He'll be voted in as the next President and I've asked that he and the club watch over you two girls after I'm gone."

"Oh Uncle, don't be silly, you're not going anywhere," she knew the words weren't true, but she wasn't ready to face the truth just yet.

"Let me finish. My will is in the top drawer of your father's old desk. I don't have much, but everything I have belongs to you and Jess. Alex I want you to know I've lived a full life with many happy memories, but the happiest memories I have come from the time I spent with you two girls. I love you both so much. I need you to promise me something."

"Anything, Uncle."

"You are the strongest person I know, Alex. You can do or handle anything that comes your way, you've already proven that with everything you've been through. I need you to promise me that you will take care of your sister."

"Of course I will."

"I also need you to promise me that you will trust the club with anything. Those men have watched you grow and are as much your family as your father and I were. The club will protect and take care of you and so you must promise to do the same for them. Protect the club, Alex, protect our town, it's your heritage."

"I will, Uncle Jimmy. I promise you I will." Alex choked back a sob as she made a promise she didn't understand.

"I'm so proud of you, Alex. I love you so much."

Alex continued to hold her uncle's hand as he lie in his bed, his eyes were closed and his mouth was turned up into a serene smile. She watched the monitors that counted his heartbeats and measured his breath. His breathing was faint, his heart rate low, and it slowly began to cease. Alex didn't even notice when the monitors beeping ended in a long flat line, she just sat there holding her uncle's hand until Jason walked in and pulled her away.

"I'm so sorry, Alex," he said to her. He needed to find a nurse and his father, but he couldn't leave Alex alone. He reached over and pressed the "Nurse Call" button on Jim's bed and waited. The nurse arrived a few seconds later. "Will you please go get my father?" He asked the nurse. "He's in the waiting room down the hall with this man's younger niece."

The nurse left the room and ten minutes later came back with Ron following behind. Alex fell into Ron's strong arms as the tears finally came to her eyes. He held her while he walked her out of the hospital room and down the hall to the waiting room. The rest, to Alex, became a blur. Someone had already told Jesse, who was now crying on Sara's shoulder. The rest of the club arrived at the hospital within minutes to help with all of the arrangements. Sara took the girls home and made them eat some food and eventually got Jess to go to bed. Alex refused to go to sleep and instead stayed on the couch until Sara left. Two days later there was a funeral for her Uncle Jimmy. He was buried in the Lion's cemetery plot next to his grandfather, father, and late brother and sister-in-law. There were several other grave markers for old club members from Alex's great-grandfather's time and some from her grandfather's time, none of which Alex knew. There weren't actually any people in this plot that Alex knew aside from her own mother and father, and now her uncle. The service for her uncle was simple. When it was over each club member threw a handful of dirt into the grave, as was custom, followed by the family members of the deceased and then the rest in attendance.

Alex threw her handful of dirt over her uncle's coffin and then left the gravesite. She disappeared for the rest of the day; Jim's motorcycle was missing from the driveway to Alex's house. The club spent the rest of the day searching for her all over town, but no one could find her. Jason knew where she went, there was only one place he could think of that she would go to, but he didn't go looking for her until later in the day. He knew that she just needed time away from everyone; time to think.

There was a cliff five minutes outside of town that Jason and Alex had found when they were young. They had to hike into the woods a bit to get to it, but it wasn't a very long hike. The first time they had found it they were riding their bicycles around town looking for an adventure. They decided, after not finding anything exciting to do, to go exploring the perimeter of the town. When they reached a hiking path they stopped to take a break, leaving their bikes concealed in the bushes. They hiked for a few minutes before the trail just ended on the edge of a cliff that overlooked the ocean. There were giant rocks and boulders all around them. Alex climbed the tallest one she could and sat on the top. Jason a little more wary eventually followed her up and the two of them sat there for hours. It became their favorite place, and they would go there every chance they got. That was where Alex had to have gone.

They hadn't been there in weeks, during the chaos of Jim's heart attack and hospitalization, but this was the only place that they could go to escape life, especially for Alex who had been through a lot in the past few years. Jason rode his motorcycle to the hiking trail, which took less time to get there than it used to when they had to ride their bicycles. He parked his bike at the edge of the woods and got off. He didn't see Jim's bike right away; he had to search for it in the bushes, but there it was. Parked in between the two bushes where they used to hide their bicycles was Jim's old motorcycle. A scary thought popped into Jason's head then: What if Alex came here to jump? He hadn't thought of that before. Jason broke out into a run and didn't stop until he reached the cliff face.

"Alex!" He called over and over again. There was no response, only silence. He screamed her name as he searched everywhere. He couldn't find her anywhere. He walked to the edge of the cliff and peered over afraid of what he might find. The ocean crashed against the bottom of the cliff face, attacking the rocks below. There was nothing down there. Jason gave up and sat down with his feet hanging over the edge. Now he was scared. He realized there was still one place he hadn't checked. He stood up and made his way over to the giant boulder Alex climbed the first time they ever came here. It took a lot of effort for him to reach the top, but when he did he was rewarded with the sight of Alex's back. She was sitting in a hunched position with her arms wrapped around her knees. He walked until he was beside her and could see her face. Her eyes were red and swollen from crying, but she was calm. She just sat there staring out over the water not noticing Jason as he sat down beside her, his arm brushing against hers.

"I was yelling your name," he said.

"I know," she replied in a quiet, raspy voice that was worn out from crying.

"You didn't answer."

"I'm sorry." She still would not look at him, her eyes scanning the ocean. They sat in silence for a long time before she spoke again. "I needed to get away from everyone, just for a little while."

"I know," Jason said.

"Uncle Jimmy said something to me before he died. He sent Jess out of the room like he knew it was coming and he had to talk to me before it was too late. He made me promise him to take care of Jess and to trust the club with anything that I need."

"He knew that the club would take care of you."

Alex nodded, "His words were 'the club will protect and take care of you so you must promise to do the same for them.' He said, 'Protect the club, Alex, protect our town, it's your heritage.'" She turned to Jason, "What did he mean?"

Jason didn't respond; he didn't know what Jim meant. Instead he sat there with her quietly, both of them lost in their own thoughts.

"You know, I knew that you would come here," he said. "Everyone's been spending the day looking for you, worried about you, but I knew you'd be here. I didn't tell them because I knew that you needed some time to be alone. Some time to think about things without people watching you, so I let you be. When I got here and found your bike, though, I began to think. I was afraid that I left you here too long and that you jumped." He looked at her before he continued, "I screamed your name, Alex. I looked everywhere for you and you never said a word. You scared the life out of me, the same way you've scared everyone else by running away. How do you think your sister feels right now? She's only twelve, Al and she's lost her mother, her father, and now her uncle. Is she going to lose her sister too?"

The tears came back to Alex's eyes as Jason said that last part to her. She stood, hiding her face from him, trying to wipe away the tears. Frustrated she turned back to him, "You're right Jason. I came here to be alone so that I could think about what to do now. I did think about jumping. I stood on the edge of that cliff for so long I'm surprised I didn't fall in. The only thing that kept me from doing it was Jesse. I thought of her and I thought: I can't leave her to deal with this on her own. Then I thought of you and your parents and how it would hurt them just as much as it would hurt Jess. I couldn't make myself leave you all like that; I couldn't make myself give up. But, how am I supposed to take care of my sister if I can't even take care of myself? Look at me Jason. Do I look like I'm ready for this responsibility? You know the club bought the house so that we can still live there. I'm nineteen years old, I've only been out of high school for a year, and now I have a house and a child to take care of. I'm working as a waitress. I'm not in school. How am I supposed to handle all of this?"

"The same way you've handled everything else: by taking one day at a time and dealing with things as they come. You can't change everything that's happened to you, but you can control what *will* happen to you in the future. You don't need a job, you own the bar and garage, but you want to work? Let's go find you a great job, better than waitressing. You need someone to take Jess to school? Then call someone to give her a ride. You want to go to college? Well let's go back and enroll you for classes this fall. You can do this, Alex. You don't need help from anyone."

"I feel so alone, Jason."

"Name one time in your life when you've been

truly alone." He waited. "You've never been alone and you never will be. I'm right here, Alex and so is the club. My parents, the guys and their families, none of them are ever going to let you feel alone. Deep down you already know that; you're just scared and that's ok. You're supposed to be scared and worried, but you've had the entire day to yourself to be scared and now it's time to snap out of it. Go back home and take care of your sister. She needs you now more than anyone." Jason was standing behind her now. He waited for her to turn, and when she finally did he opened his arms for her to fall into. "I'm right here, Alex," he whispered into her ear as they stood in an embrace.

She pulled away, wiped her face, and nodded her head, "I'm ready to go back now." They walked back down the trail together then climbed onto their bikes and rode back into town. They pulled into Alex's driveway a little after 7:30. Sara and Jesse came out of the house followed by some of the other club wives. Sara didn't ask any questions, she just pulled Alex into a hug and walked her into the house.

Alex turned away from her long enough to whisper a "Thank you" to Jason and then she was pulled inside. Jason sat in her driveway for a few minutes contemplating following her in, but decided against it. She was in good hands now; he had done everything he could for the day. Instead he rode his bike over to the clubhouse to tell the guys that she was home and she was safe.

Chapter 3

Alex stepped out of the shower, getting an instant chill before she could wrap herself up in a towel. She had been in the shower for 30 minutes and was now running late. She needed to start getting ready so she could get Jess out of bed and dressed before Sara came to pick her up. Jess had just recently turned 14 and already she was like all young teenage girls who took forever to get ready in the morning. Her sister would monopolize the bathroom for an hour sometimes trying to get her hair and her clothes to look good. Recently she had begun wearing a little bit of make-up and that had dramatically increased her mirror time. Alex had never been like that and her uncle had blamed it on the fact that she was constantly surrounded by men. Alex wore make-up sometimes, but it didn't take her nearly as long to put it on. This morning she decided against make-up entirely. Alex went down the hall and into her sister's room a little after 7:00. Still wrapped in a bath towel, she leaned over her sister and kissed her on the forehead.

"Hey you," she whispered. "It's time to get up."

"No," Jesse rolled over and put her pillow over her head.

"Come on, wake up. What would you like for lunch today?"

"I don't need a lunch remember? We are going on a field trip to the zoo today."

"Well then, what would you like for breakfast?"

"Scrambled eggs and toast?"

"Alright, but you have to get out of bed now if you want to eat before Sara gets here."

"Fine," Jesse grumbled as she crawled out of bed and went into the bathroom. Alex left Jesse's room and went into her own. She quickly threw her pajama bottoms and tank top back on and went into the kitchen to make breakfast for both of them.

"Jess, breakfast is almost ready, hurry up," Alex yelled a few minutes later.

"I'll be out in a minute," Jesse called back.

Alex poured two glasses of orange juice and set them on the kitchen table, "Come on Jess, breakfast is on the table and Sara should be here any minute now." Breakfast wasn't quite ready yet, but Alex knew it would help get Jesse moving faster. Alex put two pieces of buttered toast and a heaping scoop of scrambled eggs on a plate for Jesse. Then she made a plate for herself and put both on the table.

"Jess..."

"I'm here, I'm here." Jesse said rushing into the kitchen with her shirt only pulled halfway on.

"It's about time," Alex smiled at her sister. They both sat down and started eating. "So are you excited about going to the zoo today?"

"Yea it's gonna be cool. Valerie is going to, so it'll be fun." Valerie was Jess's best friend. Her father's name was Russell and he had been a member of the Lions for as far back as Alex could remember. He was married to a woman named Carla, who was a ton of fun and constantly helped watch Jesse when Alex needed her to. Russell and Carla had two girls; Valerie was the same age as Jess and in the same class and their other daughter Rita, was only one year behind. The three girls got along great, which definitely made Alex's life a little easier.

"Do you need anything for the field trip?" Alex asked.

"No, I don't think so. Actually…"

"What?"

"Well I think we might be going into the gift shop while we're there," Jesse looked at her older sister with a mischievous grin.

"Would you like some spending money? Never mind. Why did I ask?" Alex left the table and went into her bedroom to find her wallet. She didn't have much cash in her wallet, but she could always stop by the ATM on the college campus if she needed to. She grabbed the $15 from her wallet and went back into the kitchen. "Here take this. It's all the cash I have right now. Will it be enough?"

Jesse sighed, "I guess I'll make do." She folded the cash Alex handed her and slid it into her back pocket.

"Alright, finish your breakfast before Sara

gets here. I have to start getting ready for class." The girls finished their eggs and cleaned up breakfast just as Sara pulled into their driveway.

"Hey girls," Sara called in as she came through the front door. "Jess, are you ready?"

"Yeah I'm ready. Guess what, Sara?"

"What?"

"We're going on a field trip to the zoo today."

"I heard. That's going to be fun."

"Yeah, I can't wait. You know they have a gift shop there?"

"Oh, do they? Would you like some money to buy something special for yourself?"

"No, Auntie, you don't have to give me any money. Unless you want to, of course."

"Of course," Sara smirked and reached into her purse.

"No!" Alex yelled from the kitchen. "I already gave her money, Sara."

"I know. I was planning on giving her some anyway. How's $20 sound, Jess?" Sara handed the bill over to Jess, who quickly put it into her pocket.

"Thanks, Auntie Sara."

"You're welcome."

"You really shouldn't spoil her like that," Alex said as she came out of the kitchen to say goodbye. "It only makes her worse."

"Don't be silly. Spoiling you girls is what I'm here for."

"I'm running a little late, so I need to get moving." She turned to Jess, "Be good today. I don't want any phone calls from your teacher."

"Yeah, yeah."

"Alright, have fun." Alex hugged her sister goodbye.

"Ok Alex, I'll pick her up from school today. We should be back by 4:00."

"Thanks, Sara." Alex hugged Sara and then headed to the back of the house to get ready.

"Oh, by the way, Jason is here," she heard Sara say.

She came back out to the living room, "What? He's early. I'm not even dressed yet."

"Don't worry, he can wait."

Alex walked out onto to the driveway barefoot in time to see Jason handing another $20 over to Jesse. "Jess, stop stealing everyone's money!" Alex called out. Jess looked back at her with an evil little grin and then got into the front seat of Sara's car. "You didn't have to give her money, you know," She said as Jason approached.

"I wanted to."

Alex rolled her eyes, "Come on in. I'm not ready yet but you can hang out for a few minutes. I won't take long."

"You told me to be here on time and here you are not even ready yet."

"Unlike you I'm not usually late. I didn't expect you to show up so early, so technically I'm not late yet."

"Whatever. Hey, I brought the bike. Thought you might want to arrive in style."

"Does that mean you're not taking me?"

"Ha, ha, very funny. Just go get dressed."

She left him in the living room and went into her bedroom to get ready. Because he brought the motorcycle today, she had to change what she had planned on wearing. Despite the fact that it was pretty warm outside, she put on a pair of jeans. It was too hot for jeans, but her classes would be cold and shorts were too uncomfortable to wear on a bike. She picked out a tank top to wear that matched her jeans. This was definitely one of her favorite tops to wear. It was a black, spaghetti strapped tank top that had lace across a sweet heart neck line and across the bottom edge. The top was made from a stretchy material that was snug around her body. She brushed her brown, curly hair and with one final look in the mirror she left her room picking up her backpack, purse, and long, gray sweater.

"Ok I'm ready."

"It's about time. Do you really need all that stuff?" Jason asked as he looked up at her. Alex took her purse and crammed it into her half empty backpack. She put on her sweater and looked back at Jason.

"I only have one bag," she said. "Let's go. I can't be late again." She led the way out of the house and then locked the door behind them. Jason reached the bike before Alex and was already sitting on it by the time she got there. He held out the extra helmet he had brought for her, but pulled it back before she could take it.

"What?" She asked. He was looking at her funny.

"Are you really going to wear that?"

"What's wrong with my clothes?"

"Don't you remember what happened at the bar last weekend? You were wearing that shirt."

Alex did remember what had happened at the bar. She was working there on Saturday night, as usual. Some guy came into the bar and started hitting on her. Alex was used to drunk guys and usually was able to just ignore them, but this guy was persistent. She finally asked him to leave her alone and he refused. She got fed up with the guy and asked Dennis, the regular bar tender, to get rid of him. Dennis told the guy to beat it, but he again refused. A few minutes later Alex walked by him and he grabbed her arm. He pulled her so that she was facing him.

She wasn't exactly sure what was going through this guy's mind, but just as she was about to punch him in the face she saw Jason come up behind him. She was able to break free from the man in time for Jason to grab him and pin him down to the floor. The music in the bar stopped, and everyone was staring at the commotion. By that time every member of the club was standing around the three of them. Bobbie and Russell picked the guy up and dragged him out of the bar.

"How do you remember what I was wearing that night?" Alex had totally forgotten she had been wearing this shirt and thought it was strange that Jason remembered.

"You get me into a bar fight and you think I don't remember why? You've got to stop wearing stuff like that when you're working in the bar."

"Oh please. That was not a bar fight. The guy was completely drunk and went down the second you hit him, you can't call that a fight, I could have taken him myself. Anyway, I had everything under control before you came along. Stop acting like a girl."

"Maybe *you* should *start* acting like a girl."

"Just shut up and take me to class." Alex climbed onto the back of the motorcycle with her backpack on her back and her arms holding onto Jason's sides. Jason's motorcycle was a 1996 Harley Davidson Softail Bad Boy with a 1337cc, 5-speed, and V-twin engine. It was a collector's bike painted in glossy black with yellow, scalloped stripes. Jason loved his bike and even more than that he loved it's speed. The bike's top speed was 112 miles per hour and Jason liked to ride as close to that speed as he could.

It was only a 10 minute ride to the college from her house in the middle of town. Jason sped down the road, weaving in and out of traffic, arriving at the college in seven minutes instead of ten. Still, there wasn't much time for Alex to get to her class all the way across campus from where Jason would have to drop her off. She had been late too many times this month and couldn't afford to be late again. Jason seemed to realize this without her telling him because when they reached the parking lot he jumped the bike up onto the sidewalk. He rode down the sidewalk, narrowly avoiding the students who were hurrying to their own classes. One of the students on the sidewalk was their old friend Donnie who was on his way to class walking with his back to them. He hadn't noticed the motorcycle or the people scurrying quickly out of their way and continued to walk down the center of the sidewalk. Finally, the sound of the engine must have alerted him because Donnie turned around in time to see Jason swerve the motorcycle as close as he could to Donnie without hitting him. Alex reached out and pulled the notebook Donnie was carrying right out of his hands as they sped by.

"Hey! Come on guys! I need that for class." Donnie yelled after them. Alex turned around on the bike and waved to him. "Very funny," she heard him yell again.

Jason and Alex were both laughing; picking on Donnie had been one of their favorite past times since they were kids. Donnie loved computers and technology, but was not your average computer nerd. He was actually a jock in Middle and High school playing on both the football and basketball teams. He was over six feet tall and as skinny as a rail, and constantly wore his hair in a giant, frizzy afro. Donnie was a little clumsy and very silly, which made him an easy target for practical jokes. He spent a lot of time hanging out with the guys in the club, even helping them with computer issues from time to time, but he never asked to become a member. Alex had never seen him ride a motorcycle or even attempt to and attributed that to his clumsiness; she thought he was afraid to try. Donnie was also attending classes at the Community College, but Alex and he didn't have any classes together. He was majoring in some technology course and Alex stayed as far away from those classes as possible. She thought technology was cool, but could never wrap her head around all it entailed. She was grateful, though, that she knew someone who could easily fix her laptop whenever it crashed, which seemed to happen a lot more often than it should.

Jason didn't stop until they reached the bottom of the steps leading up to Alex's first class.

Everyone's eyes were on Alex as she got off the motorcycle, including her friends who were waiting for her at the top of the steps.

"Thanks for the ride Jason," Alex said. She was embarrassed as she noticed everyone staring. Being a part of the Fu Lions meant she was used to being stared at, but up until this moment she had been keeping a low profile at the college. Out of the corner of her eye she could see one of the guys from her class, Nate, heading towards them.

"Great," she muttered under her breath.

"What's wrong?" Jason asked.

"Nothing. I'll see you later, Jason." She turned to walk away, but it was too late, Nate had already made his way over to them.

"Hey, Alex," he said. "What's up?"

"Hey Nate." Of all the people that could have come up and talked to them it had to be Nate, she thought to herself. His full name was Nathan, but no one ever called him that. Jason and Nate were both strikingly good looking with medium builds and dark features. The biggest difference between them was the color of their eyes; Nate had light brown eyes that made every girl melt at the sight of them, but Jason had the darkest blue eyes Alex had ever seen and she couldn't help but notice them every time he looked at her. Nate was a decent guy who shared several classes with Alex and her friends. The reason Alex was nervous about his approach was because in the last month Nate had taken Alex out on two dates, which she failed to mention to Jason. Jason always got upset when Alex kept secrets from him. As Nate got closer to where she was standing, her heart began racing. She didn't need Jason causing a big scene at her school, and she knew he would if Nate mentioned anything about their past dates.

"Let's go, I'll walk you to class," Nate said. He nodded to Jason and said, "Nice bike, man."

"You ride?" Jason narrowed his eyes at Nate.

"Yeah, I've got the 2011 Harley Nightster." Alex had seen Nate's motorcycle in the parking lot before. It was a sleek, powerful bike painted glossy black with lime green flame details down its length. There was something almost spooky about his motorcycle which sometimes made Alex feel uneasy. Nate looked at Alex, "Where's your car?"

"It's at the garage," Alex replied.

"Hey, do you need a ride to the studio later?"

"No..."

"I'm taking care of it," Jason cut in.

"Sorry I was just trying to help out," Nate said.

"Thanks, but I've got it covered."

"Actually guys," Alex stepped between them. "Wendy's going to give me a ride later. I called and asked her last night." Alex turned to Nate and said, "Hey Nate, I need to talk to Jason for a sec. Go ahead, I'll catch up."

"You're going to be late again. Professor Jones isn't going to be happy," Nate said.

"Why don't you mind your own business?" Jason started to say something else, but Alex stepped in front of him.

"I'll just be a minute, Nate." When she was sure Nate couldn't hear them anymore, she turned back to Jason. "What is your problem?" She asked him.

"What?"

"Nate was only trying to be nice and you jumped all over him."

"I don't like him."

"You don't even know him, Jason."

"I don't like that he just assumed that I wouldn't give you a ride later. He acted like I wasn't even standing here."

"He did not. All he did was ask if I needed a ride."

"I don't trust him. He looks like he's trying to hide something."

"Stop being ridiculous."

"What's your deal with him anyway?"

"What? Nothing. What are you talking about?"

"You're seeing him aren't you?"

"Define 'seeing.'"

"I knew it."

"Fine. I'm not 'seeing' him alright. But even if I was, what's it to you?"

"You're kidding me right? Him? I can tell you're lying. How many times have you been out with him?"

Alex sighed, "Only twice."

"So, what are you like dating now?"

"No! I don't know, ok? I haven't decided yet." She looked down at the digital clock on her cell phone. "Great, I'm late now. Thanks a lot, I gotta go." She turned to walk away, but then stopped. "Hey Jason, I actually do need a ride home later, after I teach tonight."

"What time?"

"I should be done by 5:30."

"There's a club meeting later this afternoon, but I should be done in time. I'll come by and get you."

"Thanks Jason. I really gotta go now, see ya."

Alex ran up the steps into building. She was late to class for the fourth time this month and knew her Professor was going to be upset. Jason waited until Alex was in the building before pulling away on the bike.

Chapter 4

"What happened this morning with Nate and Jason?" Alex's friend Wendy asked as they sat down at their usual table in the small cafe next to campus, with their friend Ana. The three girls usually sat in the three big, cushioned chairs that were positioned around a small table in the far corner of the cafe. It was 10:00 in the morning and there were no classes on campus. This time was reserved for the teachers to meet with students or prepare for their next few classes and the students used it as an extra study hour. Alex and her friends also used it as their lunch hour because they didn't have another break until much later in the afternoon.

"Yeah, it looked like they were arguing," Ana added. Wendy and Alex had known each other for a long time. They had grown up around the corner from each other and had gone to school together since kindergarten. Wendy was Alex's best friend aside from Jason. They met Ana when they started attending the college. Ana lived in one of the small towns not too far away, but spent a lot of time with the girls.

"Not really," Alex replied. "I don't know what Jason's problem is lately. He's been so defensive. First the fight in the bar last week and then today with Nate. Nate offered to give me a ride to the studio after classes today and Jason said he was taking care of it."

"So, who won?" Ana asked smiling.

"Neither of them. I told them Wendy was going to drop me off later." She looked at Wendy, "You don't mind do you?"

"Sure, but I don't know why you didn't just let Jason take you."

"Because I'm sick of his attitude. He can't just jump down every guy's throat when they're trying to be nice to me."

"You are so blind, Alex," Wendy said.

"What? What are you talking about?"

It's obvious Jason likes you."

"No he doesn't. He's just acting…"

"…Jealous," Wendy finished. "Come on,

Alex, think about it. You guys grew up together. You've been best friends your entire lives. Trust me I've known you guys my whole life too and it's so obvious."

"I grew up with you too and I don't think you're madly in love with me."

"I didn't say he was madly in love with you. Are you telling me that you've never even thought about it?"

"He's hot," Ana said.

"No, I haven't," Alex said.

"Well, why not?" Wendy asked. "He's hot, he's nice, and he likes you."

"He's really hot," Ana said again. Both girls looked at her, Wendy raised her eyebrows and sipped her coffee as Alex spoke again.

"Wendy, he doesn't like me. He's like my brother, it would be so weird."

"A hot brother," Ana mumbled.

"Can we please stop talking about this?"

"Fine," Wendy said, "but I still think you're completely blind."

"Hey Alex, would you mind if I asked him out?" Ana asked.

"What? NO! Why would you want to ask him out."

"He's hot."

"So you've said," Wendy said. "Hmmm, sounds like Alex is getting a little defensive. Wasn't that what you were complaining about Jason for?"

Wendy and Ana exchanged smiles over their cups of coffee.

"So Wendy, since we're talking about boys, have you seen Sean lately?" Alex asked smugly.

"Who's Sean?" Ana asked.

"You mean Wendy never told you?" Alex asked rhetorically. "Sean is another guy who grew up with us. He has a twin sister named Elise and is best friends with Jason. The five of us have gone to school together since we were in kindergarten. Anyway when we got to high school Wendy and Sean realized that they were madly in love and they started dating. They went out for three years."

"What happened?"

"Nothing," Wendy said.

"Sean, Elise and Jason were a year older than us, so they graduated before us. When they graduated Elise decided to move into the city and their parents begged Sean to go with her, so he did."

"He just left, okay? He left and he never called me or wrote me an e-mail, nothing. He just disappeared." Wendy was visibly upset and she got up from the chair and walked away from them.

"He never called?" Ana asked.

Alex shook her head, "None of us heard a word from him until he came back a whole year later. Apparently he got into a little trouble in the city and he had to come back. Wendy hasn't gone near him since he's been back, but I know she's still crazy over him. I know that Sean still loves her too," Alex sighed. "I don't know what they're doing. They'll figure it out eventually."

Wendy came back to the table and sat back down on her chair. "Sorry," she said. "Can we please change the subject now?"

"Did you hear about Stacie?" Ana asked. The

conversation shifted to the rumors going around campus about Stacie and her new boyfriend, but Alex didn't hear a word about it. She was thinking about Jason and what Wendy said.

Alex spent the rest of her day trying to focus on her schoolwork, but it was impossible. She couldn't stop thinking about what Wendy had said. Did Jason really like her? Alex had never thought about it before. If he did, then that would definitely explain his strange behavior lately. Alex wasn't sure what to think. The rest of her classes went by in a blur. Her last class, history, ended exactly at 2:00. She and Wendy left class together and headed towards the student parking lot. Wendy was talking about something that happened in class, but Alex hadn't heard a word. She was still thinking about Jason, when they finally got into the car.

"You didn't hear a word I just said did you?" Wendy asked.

"Huh? Oh sorry, Wendy. What were you talking about?"

Wendy sighed, "Nothing important."

"You're not mad at me, are you? I shouldn't have brought up Sean that was a cheap shot."

"Yea it was," Wendy gave her a sideways glance and smiled. "No, I'm not mad. Ana didn't know the story and she would've heard it eventually. I rather have her hear it from you than someone else."

Wendy pulled out of the parking lot. "You're not mad at me, are you? I wasn't trying to push the Jason thing on you. I just think that you guys are missing something everyone else can see." Wendy asked.

"No, I'm not mad. I've actually been thinking about it all day. It kind of makes sense for us to like each other. I've just never thought about it. I mean I'm not saying I like him or anything, but I guess it's kind of weird that it's never come up between us. He's never said a word about liking me, if he does."

"Maybe he's just shy or nervous."

"Shy? Nervous? We are talking about Jason, right?"

"Well, maybe the timing hasn't been right?"

"Yeah, maybe."

The studio Alex was renting was right in the center of town. It was between the local post office and small dentist office. The public library was across the street. There was a lot of traffic in this area of town, which made it a great location for picking up new students. Wendy pulled into the parking lot that was shared with the dentist office.

"Thanks for the ride, Wendy."

"No problem. I'll see you at your cookout Saturday." Wendy waved as she pulled out of the parking lot. Alex had a lot to do tomorrow for the cookout. Today was already Thursday, and she was planning on having the entire club and their families over on Saturday. She had also invited some of her friends including Ana, Wendy, and Nate. She was a little worried about having Nate over after this morning, but it was too late now and she wasn't going to uninvite him just because Jason didn't like him.

Alex paused to rummage in her purse for the key to the studio door. Her keys had fallen into the very bottom of her bag, but she never got a chance to pull them out. When she reached the door to her studio it was already open. Alex never would have left that door open and she definitely locked it the last time she was here. Instead of pulling out her keys, she took out her cell phone and then slowly made her way into the studio.

The small waiting room, in which her students would enter first, had been completely torn apart. The chairs and end table were thrown around and were lying in various places on the floor. Magazines, coloring books, and the case of crayons were scattered across the entire floor. Her plants had been smashed leaving dirt and shards of pottery everywhere. Paintings and a mirror had been ripped from their places on the walls and torn into pieces. The door that led into the back hallway with the bathroom was still closed and appeared to be untouched. She ignored that section of the studio and instead made her way into the lesson room with the piano. The door to the lesson room had been kicked down and torn off its hinges. Alex walked in further, afraid of what she was going to find. Her desk was flipped over onto its side; all the drawers were pulled out and emptied of their contents. Books of sheet music had been ripped apart and thrown around the room and someone had taken a knife to the recliner chair in the corner. The shelving unit that held all of her music looked as though it had been smashed with a hammer.

The worst damage of all, though, was done to the piano. Someone had taken pliers and pulled out all of the strings from the inside. The front legs had been chopped off so that the piano was leaning all the way forward almost completely toppled over. The keys had also been smashed with a hammer. The studio had been completely destroyed and there was no question as to who had done it. On the wall in the front waiting room, where she once had a beautiful painting of a grand piano, the culprits left a clear message in spray paint. There were no words, no explanations, just a symbol in black paint: A tall grim reaper stood holding a sickle with bony fingers. The Reaper's Sons.

Alex dialed Ron first, but there was no answer. Jason didn't answer either. She called everyone in the club, but no one was picking up their phones. Finally she was able to reach Sean.

"Sean, it's Alex."

"Hey Alex, what's up?"

"I need to talk to Ron and no one is answering their phones. Do you know where he is?"

"Yeah, they're all in a meeting right now. They decided to meet early today. Do you want me to give him a message when they come out?"

"No, Sean. I need you to go in there and hand him the phone."

"What? Are you crazy? You know I can't go in there. They'll never vote me in if I interrupt them."

"Sean, I need you to go in there, it's an emergency. Put me on speaker phone and I can explain everything to all of them at once."

"What happened?" Alex quickly described the scene at the studio.

"It was the Reapers, Sean. Just go in there. I promise you that I'll make sure they won't hold it against you."

"Alright, hang on a sec. I'm putting you on

speaker." Alex could hear as Sean knocked twice and then opened the door into the meeting room.

She heard someone say, "Sean, we're busy. You can't be in here."

"I'm sorry," Sean replied, "but it's Alex. She's on the phone and her studio has been trashed."

"Tell her I'll call her right back when we're done," she heard Ron say.

"This can't wait Uncle," Alex shouted so he could hear her through the phone's speaker.

Ron was sitting at the head of the table with Jason on his right. They were the President and Vice President of the club. Russell was in charge of the money; he sat in the chair on the left side of Ron. The rest of the club members, including Leo, Bobbie, Kip, Sam, Dennis and ten others filled in the remaining seats around the table.

"Alright Alex, what happened?" Bobbie asked.

"The Reapers have attacked the studio. They must have done it earlier today because I was just here yesterday."

"How do you know it was the Reapers?" Leo asked.

"Because they spray painted their logo all over the wall. You guys need to get down here. I don't know what to do. Should I call Vic?" Victor was the local sheriff. He was close to the club and had turned a blind eye over the years to some of their not so perfectly legal activities. He had a new partner, named Ryan, who was young and fit and also a supporter of the Fu Lions. Even though neither was an actual member of the club they still were involved in a lot of what the club did.

"No," Ron said. "We're on our way over now. Sean take the van and call Vic. We'll be there soon, Alex."

Alex was about to say goodbye and hang up when she thought she heard something behind her.

"Hang on a sec, Uncle. I hear something." Alex walked out of the lesson room and back into the main, waiting room. The door into the back hallway was wide open. "Uncle Ronnie, I think someone might still be here." She stepped towards the door, reaching into her pocket for her father's old pocket knife that she always carried.

"Alex, get out of there," she heard Jason shout into the phone. Every member of the club was standing over the phone, listening.

"Alex, leave the studio and run next door to the dentist. We'll be there in five minutes," Ron said.

"It's ok. I think they're gone." Alex was standing in the middle of the room with her back to the front door. She breathed a sigh of relief. "I don't see anyone. I must not have heard..." Her words were cut off by a hand over her mouth. Someone had come up behind her, grabbed her, and was trying to drag her out the front door. Alex screamed through the gloved hand over her mouth.

"Alex..." Kip yelled, "Alex what's going on?" Jason looked at his father, meeting his eyes. They could hear the sounds of a struggle coming from the other end of the phone. Jason was the first and the quickest to react. He ran out of the clubhouse and jumped onto his bike, peeling it out of the parking lot as fast as possible. The others followed right behind him. They needed five minutes to reach the studio; Jason was there in three.

Sean was the last out of the clubhouse, following the others in the club van. He continued to listen to the struggle on Alex's end of the phone. He heard her scream again. He heard loud crashes and a man cry out in pain. Then there was nothing.

Alex kicked and punched as hard as she could to get out of the man's grip. He was much stronger than her, but she knew she could outrun him if she could just break free. She had dropped the phone on the floor as the man had jumped her, but her other hand still clung to the pocket knife. He gripped her knife hand and pinned it behind her, but her left hand was still free. Pain seared through her right arm as she could feel her shoulder dislocate itself under the man's twisted grip. She screamed again and bit the hand that was covering her mouth. She reached up with her free hand and found the man's face. He wasn't wearing a mask and she was able to find his left eye quickly. She pushed her thumb into his eye as hard as she could and felt blood as she scraped above his eye with her fingernail. The man howled in pain, loosening his grip on her arm. It was enough; she managed to free her knife hand as the man reached up to cover his eye. They stood facing each other, half of his face hidden behind his hand.

He was much taller than her and was wearing a tight black t-shirt that clearly showed his defined muscles. Despite being able to see half his face, she could not make out who he was. She knew a lot of the Reapers but she was sure she didn't recognize him. He moved toward her, swinging his free arm in an arc intended to hit her. She ducked down to the floor and he missed. She felt a stinging pain in her left knee as a shard of pottery sunk itself into her skin. She stood back up to face him, anger flashing in the only eye she could see. He was closer to her now and she knew that if he swung again, he wouldn't miss. One punch from this man would knock her out and she had to stay on her feet long enough for the club to get there. The man moved, his arm raising for another strike. She chose her timing carefully and when he was within inches of her, she lashed out with her right leg and kicked him backwards. At the same time she swung her right arm holding the knife and managed to slash the side of his right leg. She was standing above him as he was bent over in pain, one hand covering his face and the other trying to stop the blood coming out of the knife wound on his leg. She still couldn't make out his face; he was covering it almost as though he didn't want her to recognize him. She took a step forward, and that was when everything went black.

The sound of a motorcycle engine is what brought her back. She could hear the loud engine in the parking lot. Her eyes were shut and she was aware that she was laying on the floor. She tried to open her eyes, but the light sent a sharp pain through her head. She was lying on top of glass and pottery shards that were pushing themselves into her arms and legs. Aside from the horrible pain she felt in her head, her shoulder and knee were on fire. She tried opening her eyes again. This time the pain wasn't as bad. She managed to sit herself up and lean her back against the wall.

"Alex!" She could hear Jason yelling as he ran his way up the sidewalk and into her studio. He ran through the door, not even noticing her sitting on the floor. "Alex! Where are you?" He was frantic.

"I'm here Jason," her voice was barely above a whisper. She had to say it again for him to hear. He turned, seeing her for the first time. Alex didn't know what she looked like, but she could feel a warm stream of blood on the side of her face. Her right arm was cradled in her lap. There were scratches all over her arms and legs from having laid on the glass on the floor. A piece of pottery was shoved deep into her left knee. Jason didn't say anything, he just stared at her. They could hear more motorcycle engines in the parking lot.

"Jason, help me up," she said. "I don't want them to see me like this, they'll freak out."

"I don't think you should get up yet," he replied.

"Just please get me off this floor."

"Fine." Jason picked up one of the fallen chairs and set it upright close to where Alex was sitting on the floor, and then he went over to help Alex up, approaching her from the right side.

"Other side, Jason. I'm pretty sure my shoulder is dislocated."

He sighed and then stepped over to her other side. He lifted her up so that she was standing and then helped her into the chair. The timing was perfect; by the time she was in the chair Ron, Kip, and Bobbie burst through the door. Leo and Sean were right behind them with the rest of the club members. No one said anything as they surveyed the scene before them. The studio was destroyed and Alex was injured.

"I'm okay," she said as Kip and Ron stared at her. She smiled up at them through the pain; she didn't want them to know how bad she actually felt. No one smiled back at her.

"Did you see who it was?" Kip asked.

She shook her head, "He attacked from

behind. When I broke loose he was covering his face with his hand. I managed to stab his leg with my knife, but that's really the last I remember. There must have been someone else with him."

"You definitely got him good," Leo said. He was squatting next to a red stain on the carpet. "That's a lot of blood. Where did you hit him?"

"His leg…his right leg I think."

"Sean, you and Leo head over to the hospital. See if anyone with a knife wound to the leg has shown up since the attack." Ron directed.

"His face will be messed up too," Alex added. "I shoved my thumb in his left eye." The group exchanged looks, Kip and Sean were laughing.

"That's my girl," Kip patted her on the shoulder. Alex winced.

"Careful Kip, she dislocated that shoulder" Jason said.

"Sorry, Al."

"It's okay. I got him worse that he got me." She lied.

Sam, another older member, walked into the

studio, "Vic and Ryan are on their way," he said holding the phone to his ear. "Vic wants to know if they need an ambulance."

"Yes," Ron said at the same time that Alex said, "No."

"You're going to the hospital, Alex," Ron said. "Don't even try to argue with me."

"But I'm fine really, just a little bruised that's all." Alex hated the hospital and did everything in her power to avoid them. The look on Ron's face made it absolutely clear that there would be no winning this argument. Leo was standing over her inspecting the side of her head that had been hit.

"Ron's right. This looks pretty bad, you might have a concussion." Leo's words were proven true a few minutes later when the EMT's arrived on the scene. Victor and Ryan walked through the studio while the EMT's took a look at Alex. They agreed that Alex did appear to have a concussion, and she also needed stitches in her knee.

"We can set your shoulder here if you want. It will probably be more comfortable on the ride to the hospital," the older EMT said. Alex nodded, despite the fact that she didn't really want the club to watch. The younger EMT, a woman, stood behind her and told her to take slow, deep breaths. The older EMT stood in front of her and gripped her right arm.

"We're gonna count to three and then I'll pull. Are you ready?" Jason came over and stood on her left, shielding her from the rest of the club members. He looked her in the eyes and offered her his hand. She took it, and nodded to the EMT.

"Alright let's start our count then," he said. "Repeat after me: One."

Alex didn't even get a chance to mutter the number one; instead she gave a small yelp as the EMT pulled on her arm, popping the shoulder back into place. The horrible sharp pain was immediately replaced with relief as the shoulder settled back into its original place.

"Al?"

"Yeah."

"You can let go of my hand now." Alex realized that she was still squeezing Jason's hand.

"Oh. Sorry Jason."

"I think we're ready here," the EMT said.

"I'll ride with you," Jason offered.

"Good," Ron said. "Jason you go with Alex. I need to stay here with Vic. The rest of the guys will follow you to the hospital. I'll be there as soon as I can. Jason, you're going to need to call you mother, tell her to pick up Jesse from school and meet you guys at the hospital."

Alex could walk, which meant she didn't have to lay on a stretcher. She and Jason sat across from each other in the back of the ambulance. Jason called his mother as soon as the ambulance pulled away. Alex could hear the panic in Sara's voice as Jason talked to her.

"Mom, she's fine. She got a little banged up, but she's ok. We're on our way to the hospital. Can you go pick up Jess and meet us there?" Jason rolled his eyes and then handed the phone over to Alex. "She wants to talk to you."

"Hey Sara."

"Oh Alex. Are you alright? I can't believe

this!"

"I'm fine auntie, I'm fine."

"You're not fine. They're taking you to the hospital."

"Only as a precaution because I might have a concussion. Uncle Ron wants you to pick up Jess and meet us at the hospital."

"Of course, of course. I'm on my way. I'll see you there as soon as I can."

Alex hung up the phone and gave it back to Jason. He was quiet for most of the ride to the hospital. Alex hated the silence but wasn't sure what to say to him.

Finally he broke the silence with a question, "Are you sure you didn't see who did this?"

"I only saw him for a second. He was covering most of his face. He was young, like our age; early twenties. His hair was short and definitely light brown or blond. He was wearing a black t-shirt that was too tight and a pair of jeans. I didn't recognize him."

"Did you see any tattoos?"

"Meaning was there a reaper tattooed on his forearm? No, there weren't any tattoos that I could see. He wasn't a Reaper, Jason. They had to have brought him in from the outside."

"Would you recognize him if you saw him again?"

"I really don't think so. Maybe." It was quiet for a minute before she added, "He was really strong." She didn't know why she said it. Maybe it was because she'd been hit in the head or maybe it was because she wanted to justify why she was unable to beat him. Either way the comment made Jason uncomfortable. She watched as he shifted in his seat.

"Was he a big guy?" He asked.

"He was a little taller than you, but he didn't look much bigger. He was tough though. It took everything I had to break free. If the second one hadn't knocked me out, the first one would have managed to anyway."

"You never saw the second one?"

Alex shook her head, "No. When I got to the

studio, I didn't even think to check if there was someone still inside. I just walked right in. I tried calling all of you, but no one answered because you had just started your meeting. Sean was the only one I was able to reach and I made him go in and interrupt your meeting. It wasn't until I was talking to you guys that I heard a noise behind me. I fought with him, broke free and that's the last I remember. I guess a second one must have come in while we were fighting. I woke up to the sound of your motorcycle in the parking lot."

The ambulance stopped in front of the emergency room at the hospital. The EMTs got out and opened the back doors. Jason jumped out first, then helped lift Alex down. Her knee was beginning to hurt really badly; the original adrenaline rush from the attack was starting to wear off. She was not regretting her trip to the hospital now. They had a wheelchair waiting for her by the door. She protested, but was forced into the chair by the woman EMT that brought her here. The EMTs left them in the hands of the emergency room nurses and made their way out for their next call. The rest of it became a blur. She knew she was being pushed down the hallway with Jason, Kip, and Bobbie right behind her. The nurses asked her all kinds of questions about her medical history. Her head was pounding. Jason answered most of the questions for her. Because she had a head injury the nurses rushed her into the back. An argument broke out when the nurses tried to force Jason, Kip, and Bobbie to stay in the waiting room.

"Family only," the nurse said.

"I'm her brother," Jason argued. The nurse was forced to give in. The others unhappily stayed in the waiting room and made phone calls to the rest of the club.

A male nurse wheeled Alex to a room where they were met by a doctor. Since Alex's shoulder had already been put back into place the doctor did a once over and decided he should take a look at her knee before giving her an MRI. The shard of broken pottery was deep in her knee, right below the kneecap. The nurse, named Josh, left the room and came back with a shot of morphine. They had to wait for the morphine to kick in before they could start working. Josh and the doctor worked together to pull out the shard of pottery, clean the wound, and give her 12 stitches.

The morphine made Alex feel warm and pain free. She found that she was exhausted from the day's events. Sleep fell over her as the doctor was putting in the last few stitches. She didn't even notice when Josh picked her up, put her back into the wheelchair, and took her to the MRI room. She needed to have a CT scan of her head done to make sure there was no extensive damage.

When she finally opened her eyes again, she was lying in a hospital bed in her own room. Kip and Sean were playing cards with Jesse at a small table in the corner. Jason was nodding off on a chair he made the nurses bring in, on one side of the bed. On the other side of the bed, Sara was reading a magazine in a recliner chair that was pushed all the way back. Alex tried to sit up, but a sharp pain in her head made her crash back against her pillows with a grunt. The noise made Sara look up from the magazine.

"There you are," she said. "We were wondering when you would wake up. How do you feel?"

"Like I've been hit in the head," Alex smiled.

"Would you like some water?" Alex nodded. "Let's sit you up then." Sara put her arm behind Alex and leaned her up against the pillows. Jason awoke and quickly sat up in his chair. By now everyone was standing around the bed. Jess crawled into the bed next to her sister and rested her head on Alex's chest. Alex wrapped her good arm around her little sister.

"Are you alright?" Jess asked her.

"I'm fine," Alex said. "I'll be fine. Look at me, Jess." Jess sat up so she could see Alex's face. "Do you remember what I promised you after Uncle Jimmy's funeral?"

"You promised that you would never leave me."

"I'm not going anywhere, Jess."

"And where were you planning on going?" Ron's voice came from the doorway where he was standing, carrying a tray of coffee and a box of donuts for everyone. "Thought you might want something better than hospital food."

"What time is it?" Alex asked.

"10:00," Sean answered. "You slept all night. The morphine knocked you out and then the nurse came back and gave you something to help you sleep through the night."

"Did you all sleep here last night?"

"I was planning to stay the night with you," Sara said, "and Jess refused to leave your side. Jason stayed over too. Kip and Sean got here a couple of hours ago."

"Come on guys, let's eat," Ron said. He brought Sara her cup of coffee and a donut while the others dug in.

"Hey is this one with all the sprinkles for me?" Kip asked.

"NO!! That one's for me," Jesse shrieked and ran over to take the donut out of the box before anyone could steal it from her.

A few hours later Alex was discharged from the hospital and sent home. She was concussion free and was ordered to rest as much as possible. When they arrived home, Sara told her that the cookout had not been canceled and declared that she would be staying with the girls overnight in order to watch them and get the house ready for the cookout. She took over everything and spent the entire day preparing the house and food. Alex wanted to cancel the cookout, but Sara said it was important for business to run as usual. The club was trying to show that it was still strong even after such a horrible attack.

Alex spent the day watching T.V. as Sara flitted from here to there getting things ready and ordering Jesse around. Wendy and Ana dropped by after their classes to check in on Alex. Apparently Jason had called Wendy that morning to let her know what had happened. The girls stayed and chatted and hung out for a couple of hours, distracting Alex so she didn't feel like she was stuck on the couch alone. The girls left promising to be at the cookout the next day. Jason and Sean showed up at 5:00 to see if Sara needed any help. Everything was mostly done, so she started to make dinner, inviting the boys to stay. The boys sat down in the living room with Alex and Jess and watched one of Jess's favorite movies. An hour later Ron came over and they all ate dinner together. Sara had made fried chicken, corn on the cob, and mashed potatoes that were absolutely delicious. Sean and Jess helped her clean up and Ron went home early leaving Jason and Alex alone in the living room.

"Feeling any better?" He asked.

"Yeah, I feel pretty good actually." She was telling the truth. The pain medication the doctor had given her was working. She was left with only a slight headache and a dull pain in her knee. The stitches were itchy and she couldn't scratch them through the bandages. "Have you heard anything from the Reapers?"

Jason shook his head, "Nothing yet. They only left their logo at the studio, but no explanation. Against Vic's advice, Dad tried calling their president earlier, but he didn't answer."

"Does Vic have any leads as to who it was?"

"There weren't any fingerprints on your stuff.

They must have worn gloves when they smashed the place. They sent the blood to the labs for DNA, but Vic says that it could take a while to get the results back, especially since this isn't a major crime."

"Meaning, because I'm still alive there's no rush."

"Basically. We'll get who did this, Al."

"I know. But what exactly did they do? Except for damaging and vandalizing my studio, they didn't do any real harm."

"They attacked you! They sent you to the hospital."

"Only because I walked in on them. If I had been ten minutes later I never would have seen them." She knew that the club was going to want to get back at the Reapers for this attack. That they would want to retaliate. She was minimalizing the attack, trying to convince Jason that a counter attack was not the right thing to do until they had more information.

"Alex, we can't let them get away with this. You know that. It shows weakness if we don't retaliate."

"It shows an even bigger weakness if you do. Think about it Jason. They were trying to provoke the club and they chose to use me to do it. Why would they think that attacking me would affect you? If you retaliate I'm sure you will walk right into a trap."

"I don't know why they attacked you, but I do know that they won't get away with it."

"I'm not saying they should get away with it. I'm saying we need to stop and think about this before we do anything that might end up with worse results."

"I need to talk to my dad."

"Tell him that I need to talk to him before he makes any plans. Tell him we can have an 'unofficial' meeting during the cookout tomorrow."

Jason nodded. They continued to watch T.V. until Sean came out of the kitchen signaling they were done cleaning up dinner and it was time for the boys to leave.

"See you tomorrow, Alex," Sean waved as he walked out the front door.

"See ya, Sean." To Jason she said quietly,

"Promise me the club won't do anything 'til I've spoken with Uncle tomorrow."

"Fine. I'll talk to him when I get home. Good night, Mom," he called into the kitchen.

"See you tomorrow Jason," Sara called back.

The three girls went to bed early; Jess and Sara because they were exhausted from the long night in the hospital and Alex because of the pain medication. Although she was feeling much better, Alex was still worn out and did not have a hard time sleeping through the night and most of Saturday morning.

Chapter 5

There were women's voices talking and laughing in the kitchen. The distinct smell of bacon and coffee slowly made its way from the stove, down the hallway, and into Alex's bedroom making her stomach growl in hunger. Carefully she eased herself out of her bed and made her way into the bathroom. She studied herself in the mirror. The right side of her head and face were badly bruised. The bruise had turned from the light green color of yesterday into a dark purple and blue. Her shoulder looked fine, but her right arm had to be wrapped up into a sling. There were small scratches and bruises down her arms and both legs. She sat down on the edge of the bathtub to inspect her knee. Her left knee was swollen and bruised around the twelve stitches it took to close the wound. She took a wash cloth and cleaned around the stitches as best as she could, the cool water soothing the incessant itching in her knee, and then she applied a new coat of Vaseline and re-bandaged the whole thing. Alex combed her hair and brushed her teeth, not sure who else was in the house and preferring to look her best when she went into the kitchen.

The voices grew louder as Alex approached the kitchen.

"There you are," Sara said.

"Alex!" Jesse jumped up and wrapped her arms around Alex's waist.

"Let her breath, Jess," Sara said. "You hungry, Alex?"

"I'm starving," she replied. Alex discovered the identity of the other voices she had heard. Audrey and Carla were both wives of other members of the club. Audrey was married to Bobbie and Carla was married to Russell. Carla's family was from Peru. She had dark skin with jet black hair and dark brown eyes. Audrey was blonde with light green eyes and pale white skin. The two of them couldn't have been more different, but through the club they had become the best of friends. They were always around to help the girls whenever they needed it. Carla allowed Jesse to have sleepovers with her own daughters, and

Audrey was always around to help pick Jesse up or drop her off at school.

"Good morning, Alex," Audrey said sipping her coffee.

"Morning, Audrey. How are you guys?"

"I was doing just fine 'til Bobbie came home Thursday night and told me what happened to you," Audrey replied.

"Russell walked in at 11:00 that night and told me everything. If it hadn't been so late, I would have rushed over to the hospital," Carla added. "I called Sara yesterday and she told me not to come, that you needed your rest, but nothing was keeping me from coming here today."

"I'm glad you're here," Alex said. Sara placed a heaping plate of eggs and bacon in front of Alex and poured her a big glass of orange juice. The three women and Jess watched as Alex gulped down every last bite of the food.

"That was so good," Alex said when she was finished. "Thanks Sara." Sara took the dirty dishes to the sink to clean them.

"We came to help Sara throw the cookout later," Audrey said. "We thought she could use the extra hands."

"We also came to see if we could make you look half decent," Carla said inspecting Alex's bruises. "You know half the town is going to be here later, along with all your friends and neighbors."

"I know, but they all know what happened by now anyway. Why does it matter what clothes I wear?"

"We need to make you look stronger and less damaged. We don't know the real reason you were attacked and if anyone shows up today that was involved, we need to show them that you've been mostly unaffected." Sara said.

"That's why I'm here," Carla said. "I'm your fashion committee for the day. We'll find you an outfit that covers most of your scratches and bruises and then I'll cover that bruise on your face with some make-up. We won't be able to hide your sling, but like you said, everybody is expecting to see you injured, so the sling will look good."

The morning passed quickly. Alex was forced to spend part of it resting on the couch and the other part of it being plucked, scrubbed and made up by Carla. Sara and Audrey cleaned the house, made Alex's bed, did the laundry, and set up the backyard for the cookout. Ron, Jason, Sean, Russell, and Bobbie all showed up at different times throughout the morning bringing things like cups, plates, utensils and other things they would need later. None of them stayed long, only dropping off their items and saying a quick hello to Alex. None of them mentioned a meeting either. Alex really hoped Jason had talked to Ron about postponing the club's retaliation plans. She was so afraid the club was going to make a mistake that would lead to more trips to the hospital.

Carla helped Alex get dressed before the guests started to arrive. Alex's shoulder was still painful and the two of them had a hard time getting her into a shirt. Carla had picked out a pair of jeans and a three-quarter length sleeved t-shirt that hid most of Alex's bruises and scratches on her arms and legs. Most of the club members arrived early. The rest, along with Wendy and Ana, would be there within the hour. Alex stepped into her backyard and made her way over to the grill where Ron was standing, getting ready to start the cooking.

"Hey Uncle Ronnie."

"Hey kiddo. Feeling any better today?"

"Yeah I feel a lot better than yesterday. Uncle Ron, I need to talk to you."

"What's up?"

"Not now, maybe later. I need to talk to you and the guys together, about a retaliation plan."

"Jason told me last night. How about we enjoy the party and afterwards we'll do a small meeting in the house."

"Thanks, Uncle."

More and more of her guests continued to arrive. The backyard was packed with people; almost everyone from the town was there. Everyone's first priority when they arrived was to check on Alex. They had all heard about the attack and were eager to hear Alex's first-hand account of the story. They all asked the same questions: "What Happened? Are you alright? Do the police know who did it? Is there anything I can do to help?" Alex quickly tired of answering these same questions over and over again. She understood, though, why the cookout had to take place: the more people saw Alex was okay, and saw that the club was continuing like normal, the better. Word would reach the Reapers that their attack had no effect on the Lions, which is exactly the way she wanted it. Jason arrived with Sean and Donnie. The three boys stopped to say hello to Alex before they started helping with some of the food. Donnie stayed with Alex until Wendy and Ana got there.

"How've you been, Donnie?"

"Pretty good. Other than the whole getting-the-crap-kicked-out-of-you-thing, how've you been?"

"Can't complain. I actually need to ask you a favor, if you don't mind?"

"Sure. What can I do?"

Alex shook her head, "Not here. I don't want anyone to overhear us. Can I stop by your place sometime this week?"

"Sure. Give me a call first and I'll let you

know if I'm around."

"Great! Thank you so much Donnie."

"No, problem."

Wendy and Ana arrived shortly before the food was served. "I feel horrible," Wendy said as she bent down to Alex, who was sitting in a chair on the patio, to give her a hug.

"Why?" Alex asked.

"I should have waited until I saw you walk into your studio before I pulled away. If I had stayed then you never would have gone all the way inside or I could have come in with you and the attack might not have been so bad."

"They would have attacked us both and you would have been in that ambulance with me. This isn't your fault, Wendy. Stop being silly."

"Hey by the way, Wendy, Sean is here," Alex said.

Wendy perked up, but then shrugged and said, "So?"

"So? So, when are you going to forgive him and ask him out again?"

"I'm not."

"Why not? You've really got to get over this. The boy only left so that his sister wouldn't be alone in the city. He came back didn't he? I know you still like him."

"So what if I do? He hasn't exactly apologized and since he's been back he's barely spoken to me."

"That's because he knows you're still angry with him. He doesn't know what to say to you."

"Sean is really hot, Wendy," Ana said.

"Don't start, Ana," Alex gave her a pointed look. "Do what you want Wendy, but this is payback for what you said about Jason the other day."

"Yeah, I knew I'd pay for that," Wendy rolled her eyes and the three girls laughed.

Jess appeared a few minutes later with a plate of food for Alex. No one was letting Alex get up out of the chair to help herself to food or to mingle. She was forced to sit in exile on the patio and wait for people to come to her. Wendy and Ana stayed with her, the three of them sitting in a row. Jesse joined them while they ate.

"I thought you invited your friend Nate," Jesse said.

"I did," Alex replied. "He must have been too busy."

"You know, I actually don't remember seeing him in class today," Ana said. "We have a morning class together and I'm pretty sure he wasn't there."

"He probably didn't want to face Jason after their little scene yesterday," Wendy interjected.

"What scene?" Jesse asked.

"It was nothing," Alex said.

"Nate offered Alex a ride after class and Jason flipped out," Wendy answered.

"He did not. Stop being dramatic Wendy."

"I'm just saying that's what happened. You know there's a rumor going around about you and him. I heard people saying when he thought you were in trouble he flew out of the club and got there before anyone else was able too."

"He did get to me first, but that's because the clubhouse was only five minutes away, and you know how Jason drives."

"I heard that he picked you up and carried you to the ambulance," Ana added.

"Don't be ridiculous, Ana. He helped me up off the floor, so I could sit in a chair. I didn't want the other guys to see me lying on the floor the way that I was."

"The point is," Wendy interrupted again, "that people are talking. They're all saying exactly what I said to you that morning. The two of you together just makes sense."

The girls continued to eat and chat. Wendy and Ana caught Alex up on some of the latest campus gossip. Some of the men from the club were gathered around the grill, Jason included, laughing and having a good time. Alex looked up at the sound of Bobbie and Kip laughing loudly. At the same moment Jason looked over to where the girls were sitting. Their eyes locked.

Jason arrived at the cookout early with Sean and Donnie. He walked out back, said hello to his father, gave his mother a hug, and sat down next to Alex. He had spoken to his father briefly the night before about what Alex had said. He hated to admit it, but he knew she was right.

"I told Dad what you said," he told her.

"I know, he told me. We're going to have a meeting when people start to leave later."

"I heard. Listen, Alex, it's killing me to say this, but I think that you're right. It's going to take a lot to convince the guys to not retaliate, and I just want you to know that I'll have your back in the meeting."

"Thanks, Jason. I'm not exactly sure what to say to them yet."

"You'll think of something." He left her on the patio with Donnie and made his way across the lawn to say hello to some of his friends. He wasn't entirely convinced, himself, that her plan was the right thing to do, but he knew that once they were in the meeting she would come up with something great to say that would persuade everyone to wait. Alex was an amazing speaker who could convince anyone to do almost anything; she could sell sand to a person if they were standing in the middle of the desert.

Alex had definitely been right when she said that she and Jesse were a weakness for the members of the club. The members all had a serious soft spot for those two girls, which was a problem. Alex especially was becoming a problem for Jason. Twice in the past week, he had jumped to her defense without even asking if she needed him to; once last weekend at the bar when that guy wouldn't leave her alone, and the morning of the attack when Nate had offered her a ride. Jason did not like Nate. That was obvious. He knew Nate was just trying to be nice when he had offered Alex a ride, but Jason didn't like that Nate just assumed she would need one. He had just dropped her off and was still standing there and Nate acted like he didn't even exist. He didn't know what it was about the guy, but something about Nate rubbed him the wrong way. Alex had dated a few guys during high school and it never really bothered Jason, but there was no way he was going to stand by and watch her date Nate. Nate was not to be trusted.

The meeting later was going to be a tough one. In normal circumstances the club would have already retaliated by now, but these were not normal circumstances. It was very rare for the Reapers to attack people outside of the Lions' club members. Depending on the seriousness of the attack, the club would come up with a plan and then execute it as quickly as possible. Retaliation attacks usually were done within two or three days of the initial attack. It was already day two since Alex had been attacked and there had been no discussions about a retaliation plan. The men would be getting itchy soon, Jason hoped Alex was in one of her inspirational speech moods.

A bunch of the club members had gathered around Ron at the grill while he cooked. Jason walked over to them.

As he approached, Bobbie called out, "Hey, there's Lover Boy." Jason didn't know who he was talking about, but after seeing the rest of the guys look his way he realized they were talking about him.

"Huh?" he said.

"They're teasing you Jason," Ron said.

"I don't get it."

"Some of the guys here are under the impression that you like Alex," Leo said.

Jason looked at Bobbie and asked, "Why do you think that?"

"Because you got to Alex the fastest."

Bobbie laughed hysterically as he said, "You should have seen yourself! You flew out of the clubhouse so fast, all that was left of you was a cartoon cut-out in the wall." The others, including Jason's father, were all laughing at him.

"And don't forget," Kip added, "he got to her first and helped her up. Then he held her hand as they popped her shoulder back in place."

"He spent the night at the hospital too," Ron said.

"Dad!"

"What? It's true."

"We're only messing' with you Jason," Bobbie said. "You two just fit together so well. How come you've never asked her out?"

"Yeah. I always wondered why not," Sean said.

Jason gave a pointed look at Sean before answering, "It's never crossed my mind."

"What? Why not? Dude, she's hot." Now everyone scowled at Sean. "Sorry," he said.

"Anyway, it's true. She's a very pretty girl," Bobbie continued. "She already knows everything about the club so you wouldn't have to worry about that. She's smart and funny and you both already know everything about each other. Look at her and tell me you don't feel anything for that girl."

Jason did look at her. She was sitting in a chair on the patio, balancing a plate of food in her lap while she struggled to eat with only one hand; her right arm was wrapped in a sling. She was wearing a long sleeved t-shirt and a pair of jeans that covered the stitches in her knee and all of the other small cuts and bruises she had received from lying on the floor of the studio. Despite the medications the doctor gave her, he could tell she was still in pain by the way she was moving, wincing every time she had to make a big movement. The bruise on her face was pale from being hidden behind make-up. This had to be the work of Carla. Jason smiled to himself as he tried to picture Carla forcing Alex to wear make-up and to dress up nice for the cookout. Alex must have hated that.

For the first time since Jason had known her, Alex appeared weak. She had always been tough, tagging along with him and his friends no matter where they went or what they did. He even forgot sometimes that she was actually a girl and had more limitations than he did. This attack only reminded him that she wasn't as strong as she tried to act. She looked almost fragile sitting in that little chair on the patio. He watched as she rolled her eyes at something Wendy said. The other three girls were laughing at something that seemed to make Alex feel uncomfortable as she shifted in her chair. He knew that he was staring too much, but he couldn't manage to make himself look away. Somewhere in the background he could still hear the guys laughing at him and cracking more jokes about him and Alex. He decided to look away and just as he started to she looked up at him. That's when their eyes locked.

Chapter 6

The club members, all 17, gathered around Alex's living room. Some were sitting on the couch, others had brought chairs in from the kitchen, and a few of the younger ones stood behind the couch. Alex was propped up on a stool in front of the television so that everyone could see her. It wasn't normal for the club to have a meeting outside of the clubhouse, but these were not normal circumstances.

Ron started, "As we are all aware, at this point, there was a direct attack on one of our family members. Although Alex is not a member of this club, I think we all agree that she is still an important part of it. She and her sister are the last direct descendants of our original founder. This attack was planned as a strike against us. This attack demands satisfaction."

There was murmuring amongst the men, followed by shouts of approval. Some even stood up shouting suggestions for getting back at the Reapers.

Now it was Alex's turn, "I have a plan," she

shouted above them, commanding their silence and attention. "Please, hear me out before you make any decisions. I was the victim of this attack, and therefore I deserve the right to choose our retaliation." There were nods of approval from some of the men. She paused and then continued on, "I propose that we do nothing."

"Alex, are you crazy?" Kip called out. "We have to retaliate."

"We have to show the Reapers that they can't get away with this," someone else said.

"We can't let them think we are weak," Bobbie said.

"If you attack now, then you'll be showing your weakness to not only the Reapers, but anyone else out there who's trying to find one," Alex said back.

"How's that?" Bobbie asked.

Alex looked over at Ron who nodded for her to continue, "Why did the Reapers attack me?" She asked them. Silence; the men were quiet as they all considered the question. "I've been thinking a lot about this," Alex continued, "and there's only one answer. The Reapers know how much my sister and I mean to the club. They know that you have all taken care of us since we were young and they know that you would do anything for us. They have to know this because why else would they have chosen me? If they just wanted to hurt the club they would have chosen one of you or one of your family members, not me. Obviously they know more about us than you think, which means that they're also expecting you to go after them. You'll be walking straight into a trap."

Alex let the information sink in. The men were quiet, no one wanting to be the first to speak up. Alex knew she was right. Jason and Ron were sitting side by side on the couch in front of Alex. Ron was waiting to see if anyone else would step up to support Alex's idea. Jason had made a promise and now it was time to honor it

"Alex is right," he stood. "It's too risky to act now. We need to take our time and make a plan. I'm not saying we shouldn't get back at them. I'm just saying that we need to do it right."

Ron said, "I didn't agree with this at first, but after thinking about it I realize it is our best option. Let's take a vote. Raise your hand if you agree that we wait for retaliation."

Leo raised his hand first, winking at Alex as he did. Kip, Russell, Sam, and Bobbie's hands came next, followed by all twelve other members. It was a unanimous vote.

"There's something else," Alex added.

Ron turned to face her with a quizzical look.

"I think whoever did this was someone who's close to us. To me. I haven't told any of you this, but the man who attacked me wasn't trying to hurt me...he was trying to kidnap me."

She paused for effect while whispers made their way from one end of the room to the other. Jason turned to face Alex, "Are you sure?" he mouthed so no one could hear. She looked into his eyes and nodded. He moved toward her but checked himself remembering that the club would be watching. Instead he moved so that he was standing beside her while she sat on her stool.

"When he grabbed me he put his hand over my mouth, and then tried to drag me out of the building. I managed to fight back, but I think the only reason they didn't put up more of a fight, and why they left me there, was because they had heard me on the phone with you."

"If that's true," Bobbie spoke up, "then the person knew what time you were going to be at the studio, which means they know your schedule. It could be anyone from town."

"We don't know that for sure," Leo said. "Everyone in town knows Alex, but they don't all know her schedule. We need to find out if anyone's been asking around about it."

"I'll ask around, see if anyone knows anything," Dennis offered.

"Me too," his brother, Sam, added.

"Well that settles it then," Ron said. "Tomorrow we'll meet at the clubhouse at 3:00 to discuss our next steps. I think that's everything, so let's clear out and let Alex get some rest."

The club members began to stand up, moving chairs back and making their way towards the door.

"Wait!!" Alex called out. "There's one more thing I need to ask of you." The men went back to their seats.

"What is it, Al?" Leo asked.

"Sean and I both want to be patched in as members."

The looks on their faces were priceless to Alex. In order to be patched in as a member of the Fu Lions the vote had to be unanimous. If the club voted yes, then the new member would receive the Fu Lions official patch to be sewn onto the back of a black leather jacket. This jacket would stand as a symbol, no matter where the person went, that they were an official member of the club. Alex had wanted to be a member of the club since she was very young and had spent her life coveting that patch. She had watched both her uncle and her father wear their jackets wherever they went. She knew what the club had meant to them both and she wanted to be a part of it. Women, however, were never patched in as members.

Despite that, Alex was determined to make herself the first woman Lion and now was as good a time as any to ask. Sean was standing in the back of the room. He had no idea that Alex was going to ask for him to be a member, let alone herself, he didn't know what was going through that head of hers.

"What?" Ron asked.

"Sean and I want to be patched. Sean has been working his butt off for this club for months. He's more than proven his loyalty to the club, especially this week. He's afraid he hurt his chances by interrupting your meeting Thursday, but if he hadn't then I'd be a lot worse off. He deserves to be patched in."

Ron studied Alex for a minute. "Sean, come up front," he said. "Did you know about this?"

"I had no idea," Sean replied.

"I never said anything about this to him," Alex said.

"Is anyone opposed to taking a vote on Sean becoming a member?" Silence. "Let's take another vote then."

Ron went around the room and had each member say either "Yes" or "No." Out of the 17 club members, all of them voted yes. Sean was now an official member of the Fu Lions motorcycle club.

"I'm still going to put you on probation," Ron said, "because it's a lot sooner than we planned on voting you in. Welcome to the Lions. Well I think we're finished here."

"Wait, what about me?" Alex asked.

"What about you?"

"I want to be patched in too!"

"Not this again Al, let it go."

"No. I have as much right as the rest of you do. Maybe even more so, because of my family. I think I at least deserve the courtesy of you thinking it over."

"Alex it's too dangerous."

"Can't we at least see if I have a shot, by asking for a vote?"

Ron sighed, "Alright. One more vote tonight guys."

"No."

"Absolutely not."

"Not gonna happen."

"No way."

"I'm sorry Al, but I have to say no," this last from Dennis the bartender. More "No's" followed until all who was left to vote was Leo, Jason, and Kip.

"I love you Alex," Kip said, "but I can't make myself say yes. No."

"I say yes," said Leo. "Why not?" He winked at her.

"Because it's too dangerous!" Jason blurted out. "There's no way I'm voting you into this club, Alex."

"I thought you were supposed to have my back tonight."

"Yeah, when it came to your "Non-retaliation" plan." He made air quotes with his fingers as he said "Non-retaliation." "I didn't know anything about this. My vote doesn't matter anyway. Everyone else already said no."

"Your vote matters to me," Alex replied, and it was the truth. She didn't understand why, but she realized at that moment that she desperately needed Jason to approve. He'd always known how much she wanted to be in the club. The fact that he was saying no felt like a betrayal to her. She was crushed.

"I'm sorry, Al, but I'm never going to vote you in, so it's not worth arguing about."

"But it *is* worth arguing about. Why can't I be voted in? Who are you to tell me that I can't do something?"

"I'm your best friend, which is exactly why I won't vote you in. You have no idea how dangerous things can get in this club."

"So you're telling me that I can't risk my life in the club, but its ok for me to risk my life *for* the club, everyday."

"You're not..."

"You, obviously have no idea how dangerous it is for those of us on the outside. We have no idea what you guys are up to. We get threatened and attacked. We never know when we're going to get a phone call telling us one of you is dead and we never know who's next. We risk just as much as any of you do, but we're not allowed to be a part of anything that you do? How can we defend ourselves if we don't even know who our enemy is? You become our worst enemy by alienating us!"

"You're being ridiculous."

"Am I?! Think about it for a minute, Jason. Which one of us was attacked? There's an even better question to ask, considering the person who attacked me had to be someone I know. Why don't you ask: Who's next?"

"Enough!" Ron stepped between Alex and Jason before Jason could get his next words out. "Alex you're right. Our families are in danger everyday because of us. I also agree that you and sister are still in danger, so I'm going to assign someone to be with you at all times from now until we can settle this problem."

"But..."

"No arguments. You've made your points. No one is going to change their mind for you tonight. Starting tomorrow you and Jess will be accompanied wherever you go: school, work, shopping, I don't care. Someone will be there. I can't take the risk of you being attacked again, especially unprotected. It's time for the rest of us to go now. You need to get some rest. Sara will be back in the morning to check in and help clean up after this party. I'll be sending someone with her and he'll spend the day with you and Jess until we can come up with a rotation system for watching the two of you." Ron turned to go. Alex stayed where she was planted on her stool as she watched them all leave. Sean and Jason lingered behind the rest.

When everyone was gone, Sean turned to Alex and said, "I would've said yes, just so you know."

"Really?"

"Yeah, why not?"

"Thanks Sean," she smiled. She knew he was trying to make her feel better; it was working. He went to the door.

"Hey, Alex?"

"Yeah."

"Thanks."

"You're welcome, Seany," He left her as she started putting some of the chairs back into place. She noticed out of the corner of her eye that Jason was still standing in the doorway. The chairs were heavy and hard for her to maneuver with only one good arm, which was still weak.

"Here, let me help," Jason took the chair from her.

"I don't need your help." She pulled the chair back from him.

"Stop being silly, Al, let me help you."

"Haven't you done enough? You made me look childish and dumb in front of everyone, after you specifically promised me that you would back me up."

"I promised that I would back you up on your plan. I didn't know about this."

"That's not the promise I was referring to. I was talking about the one you made me when we were kids. The one when you said you would do anything to help me into the club, because nothing in the world should separate us. We're a team. I guess you forgot." Before he could respond she said, "Forget it. Just go home."

She stormed off leaving the rest of the chairs where they were in the living room and slamming her bedroom door behind her. The two of them so rarely fought that Jason felt guilty leaving her like this. He followed her to her bedroom door and raised his hand to knock. Instead of knocking he placed his open hand on the smooth surface of the door while he thought. He hadn't forgotten that promise he made to her so long ago, but things had changed. He knew what being a member meant and how hard it was. He never wanted to see her in the hospital like this again. If breaking some silly promise he made to her when they were kids was the only way to keep her safe then he was willing to do it no matter the consequences. He knew he hurt her, but he was willing to live with that for now. He leaned his forehead against the door and then forced himself to walk away. He left the chairs where they were, got on his bike, and drove away without saying another word.

Chapter 7

Alex woke up grumpy the next morning. As promised, Sara was there cleaning up from the night before and making breakfast for Jesse. Also as promised, Sean had come to spend the day with the two girls. He was sitting at the breakfast table with Jesse waiting for Sara to bring him a plate of food when he noticed Alex walk in.

"Morning Alex," he greeted her.

"So, you're the one they sent?"

"Yup. This is my first assignment as an official club member."

"Why you?"

"They figured since you fought so hard to get me voted in that you would less likely be mad at me."

"Meaning, you were the only person other than Leo that didn't say no to me last night."

"Technically I didn't even vote."

"Right. So, they figured I probably wouldn't bite your head off when you showed up this morning."

"Basically."

"Nice."

"So, what's the plan for today?"

"Alex isn't supposed to be doing anything," Sara cut in. "She still needs to take it easy, especially if she wants to go back to class this week."

"Apparently I have no plans," Alex said to Sean as she took a seat next to him at the table.

"That's ok, we can hang out here for the day. Jess was just telling me how good she thinks she is at cards. I was thinking I should challenge her to a round of poker."

"Really?" Jesse perked up. "What's the stakes?"

"No gambling," Sara cut in again. Jesse slumped in her chair and muttered something under her breath.

"Winner picks a movie to watch later," Sean said looking to Sara for approval. Sara nodded her head.

"You're on!" Jesse said sitting back up in her chair. Sara gave them each a heaping plate of eggs with bacon and toast, which Sean gulped down faster than everyone.

"Thanks for breakfast, Sara," he said.

"Don't mention it. Um where do you think you're going?" She asked as Sean tried to leave the room.

"I was gonna go watch T.V. 'til Jess was ready to play cards."

"I don't think so. You can help me with the dishes while the girls finish up." Alex and Jesse smirked to each other as Sean muttered under his breath and cleared away his plate.

The three of them played poker all morning, after Sara left. Jesse won every game but one, which Alex won. Sean didn't win any of the rounds and was forced to watch what he called "girly" movies for the rest of the day. He complained through the entire first movie, but at the end Alex caught him wiping away a tear from his eye.

Later in the afternoon Sean announced that there was a club meeting that he had to go to and the girls would have to go with him.

"No way. I'm not going." Alex was adamant.

"Come on, Al. They told me not to leave you alone for a second and I have to be at that meeting. You can come in and wait for me in the bar and then when the meeting is over you can go wait in the car so you don't have to talk to anyone."

After a lot of begging from Sean and a little coaxing from Jesse, they were able to persuade Alex to go to the clubhouse. Sean had come to their house on his bike, so Alex drove the three of them over in her car.

Sean opened his hand up to Alex, motioning to the keys. "I don't trust you," he said.

"You're kidding right?"

Sean shook his head. Alex sighed and begrudgingly handed the car keys over to Sean. She waited in the car until she knew everyone was in the meeting room before she joined her sister at one of the tables in the bar area. The meeting dragged on for almost two hours and then finally the doors opened. Alex walked out of the clubhouse and waited next to the car, since she didn't have the keys, without saying a word to anyone. Sean came out a couple of minutes later, talking to Jason. Finally Sean was ready to go and made his way over to a very unhappy Alex. Jason contemplated following Sean over to say hello to the girls, but stopped when he saw Alex glaring at him. If looks could kill, Jason thought, then he would be dead.

Before Sean could hand the car keys back to Alex, Ron came out of the clubhouse and motioned to her to join him. She was reluctant to talk to him, but knew she wouldn't be able to avoid him or the others forever.

As she approached Ron said, "I know you're angry about last night and the last thing you want to do is talk to me. I don't blame you, but please let me say what I need to say, Alex. Please trust me."

"Fine," Alex grumpily replied.

Ron pointed to the two stone lions that stood outside the clubhouse entrance, "Tell me what you see."

"What do you mean?"

He pointed to the lions again, "Describe them to me."

"They're two stone lions. What about them?"

"Keep looking."

Alex sighed, "This doesn't make any sense, Uncle. What do you want me to see?"

"I want you to look closely and describe each one to me. Start with that one," Ron pointed to the statue on the right.

"Alright, fine," Alex stepped in front of the statue on the right and began to describe it. "It's a white stone statue of a male lion with its mouth half open. The lion is standing upright and holding down a ball with its front paw."

Ron nodded, "Good. Now this one," he indicated the second figure.

"This one's the same. It's a white stone lion. The only difference is this one has its mouth closed and it's playing with a lion cub with its front paw."

"You're missing something. Look closer."

Alex stared at the statue quietly for a few seconds, "I don't see anything."

"Look closer."

"There's nothing else."

"Closer."

Alex was getting frustrated, "I don't see it, okay? I don't know what I'm supposed to be looking for and I don't understand why you're making me do this!"

"Alex Murphy, don't you dare raise your voice to me. You need to look harder for the differences in these two statues."

"I already told you the differences! This one has its mouth closed, is playing with a cub, and is a female..." Alex slapped a hand over her mouth. "This is a female lion. How could I have missed that?"

"Because you weren't looking for it. You assumed, just like everyone else, that because these lions are symbols of guardianship and power that they were male. I know your father told you about the founding of our club, but did he ever tell you why your great-grandfather picked the lion as our symbol? Or more specifically why the Fu Lions?"

"My father told me it was because the Fu

Lions from Chinese lore had special mythical powers that they used to ward off evil spirits."

Ron nodded, "That's one reason. The Fu Lions, which are also called Foo Dogs, were commonly placed outside the entrances to important buildings like temples and palaces. They guarded these buildings and the people inside from 'evil spirits,' much like we protect and guard our town and the people who live here. That's where our name comes from, but that wasn't the only reason Killian Murphy chose the lion.

"The lion is a symbol of strength and power. They are known to be aggressive and are called the 'King of the Jungle' or the 'King of the Animal Kingdom.' They are dangerous and other animals do their best to stay away and avoid lions."

"That doesn't explain why my great-grandfather put a male and female outside of the clubhouse."

"The Fu Lions were always placed in pairs. Both the male and the female had their own responsibilities when it came to guarding people. The male lion's job was to guard the building itself. His mouth is open because his roar would scare away the evil that was trying to get inside. The female lion was the protector of the people who were within the building. The cub she is playing with is supposed to stand for the cycle of life. Just like in a real lion pride, the male lion will fight to protect his pride from predators and the female lion will raise and protect her family from within, by providing food and by caring for the cubs."

"You know an awful lot about lions, Uncle," Alex grew amused the more Ron spoke.

Ron laughed, "I know. I did a lot of research on lions a few years ago, after a discussion I had with your father and uncle."

"What discussion?"

"They came to me one day because they wanted to ask me a favor. I was their best friend my whole life and they needed my support for a proposal they wanted to present to the club," Ron paused and sighed. "They wanted you to become a member when you were old enough to join."

Alex gasped, "They what?"

"They told me this story about how male lions couldn't function on their own without a female and how the Fu Lions were always in male and female pairs. They said the fact that Killian Murphy had placed a female lion outside the clubhouse meant that he believed in all of the Fu Lion legends and because of that they believed he wouldn't object to having a woman become a member. They also said that a Murphy would always belong at the head of our meeting table no matter if they were a boy or a girl. You and your sister are the only heirs the Murphy's have and they believed the club belonged to you. They made me promise to support their decision and to help you become a member."

"And did you?"

"I did. I swore I would do whatever I could to help you. They convinced me it was the right thing to do, but I told them they would have to wait until you were at least eighteen or else I wouldn't help them. Your father was killed a year later, Alex. The day your Uncle Jimmy died he called me to his side before you got to the hospital. He reminded me of my promise and asked that I stay true to my word. I had every intention of helping you Alex, but after Jimmy died I didn't think you were ready. I didn't want you to have to worry about anything, so I kept quiet. I became selfish, didn't want you in the club. I wanted to protect you and your sister and keep you both as far away from danger as I could. I love you girls like my own children, Alex. I realize now that it was wrong. You were ready and you needed the club to help you through those bad times. But I also realized something else, the club needed you even more. You're smart, Alex, and you're strong. I never got the chance to vote last night and I'm sorry that I didn't. I would have said yes. I broke my promise to your family, so I'm going to make you a new one. I promise you that I will do everything in my power to make you a member of the club. Now I need you to promise me something."

"Anything," the word came out breathlessly.

"You need to promise me that no matter what happens you will never give up on the club. Promise me that you will fight to protect our town and the people in it."

Alex smiled, "You know, Uncle Ronnie, I already made that promise once before. The day Uncle Jimmy died he held my hand and made me swear that I would never turn my back on our town or the club. That as the only Murphy old enough, it was my duty to protect the town and help the club. I promise you that I will stick to my word and I will honor my family's legacy."

Ron hugged Alex, "I believe you will," he whispered in her ear. A car horn went off behind them. Sean and Jesse were waiting for Alex in her Maxima and Jesse was getting restless.

"Come on, Al," Jesse yelled out the window.

"Go on," Ron said. "Go home and rest. We'll talk again soon." He paused and then added, "I love you, kiddo."

"I love you too, Uncle." Alex joined her sister and Sean in the car and Ron watched as they drove away.

Sean spent the night in the guest room. It felt weird to Alex to have three people in the house again. It had been at least two years since anyone had slept in that room. Originally it had been her room, but after her father and her uncle died, she took over the master bedroom. The master bedroom was slightly bigger than her old room and had a much nicer closet. Alex thought that Jesse would want to move into Alex's old room because it was bigger than the one Jesse was in, but Jesse loved her own room and refused to leave it. The extra room was going to be getting a lot more use over the next few weeks since the club was determined to keep the girls under 24 hour surveillance. Sean and Kip were assigned to spend the most time with the girls since neither of them had families or jobs other than working at the clubhouse. Sean still lived at home with his parents, and sometimes spent his nights at the clubhouse in one of the extra downstairs rooms, so he would be staying with the girls for the next couple of weeks. Jason was the only other member that was single who had the availability to guard the girls, but since Alex and Jason weren't exactly getting along, he wasn't assigned to guard either of them.

Monday was a much harder day to get through than Sunday. Jesse had to go to school, so Sean was assigned to take her and Kip spent the day with Alex. Kip showed up at the house in time for Sean to get Jesse to school. It took a lot of convincing, but both Alex and Jesse's schools were going to permit one person to stay with them during the day. Neither of them wanted any trouble nor did they want to be liable if something happened, so they allowed the extra protection.

Alex loved Kip and had known him her whole life, but his presence irritated her throughout the day. She was still supposed to be taking it easy, but she desperately needed to get out of the house. Eventually she was able to persuade Kip to take her to the grocery store. There wasn't much food left in the house after the cookout and now Alex was going to be responsible for feeding three people every night, sometimes four. Kip helped her shop, lifting the heavier items and reaching the higher shelves that

Alex couldn't. He even picked out some snacks that he wanted to have when he was at the house. He paid for all of the groceries, against Alex's will and he helped her put them all away when they got home. Jesse and Sean were home by 3:30 and Alex started cooking an early dinner, inviting Kip to stay. He protested until she mentioned that she was going to make fried chicken and mashed potatoes; he changed his mind and stayed for dinner. He left the house a little after seven, leaving Sean with the girls. Sean challenged Jesse to another card game, Rummy this time, and found himself watching "The Notebook" before bed. After the movie, Jesse went to bed and Sean finally took a break from the girls and got into a hot shower. Alex went to her room and packed her bag for class the next day. She couldn't wait to finally see her friends again and to breathe in some fresh air.

"Alex?" Sean was out of the bathroom and looking for Alex.

"I'm in here, Sean," she called to him. He walked down the hall and stood in her doorway.

"I'm done in the bathroom if you need it," he said.

"Ok. Thanks."

"Do you mind if I go to bed early? I'm beat."

"Jess wear you out today?"

"I forgot how much teenage girls could talk," they both laughed. "We had a fun day though."

"Yeah, Jess can definitely be a handful. Hey can I ask you something?"

"Sure."

"When are you going to ask Wendy back out?"

"What?"

"I saw you two at the cookout. I know she still likes you even though you left. You should ask her out."

"You think so? I don't know."

"She's mad at you for leaving, it still hurts her. She's been waiting for you to apologize or say something to her since you got back. What are you waiting for?"

"I don't know."

"Talk to her. Trust me."

"I'll call her tomorrow."

Alex shrugged, "Go on to bed. I'm gonna read for a little while and then head to bed myself."

"Well, I'm a light sleeper so if you need anything or someone else comes in to kidnap you just give me a shout." Judging by the loudness of his snoring the night before, Alex thought Sean was anything but a light sleeper. The reassurance was nice though.

"Alright. See you in the morning," she said.

"Night."

Alex finished packing her backpack and went into the bathroom to brush her teeth. She was feeling much better; her shoulder still hurt some and she had to take aspirin to keep away a headache, but for the most part she was beginning to heal. Most of the smaller cuts and bruises were almost completely gone. All that was left was the stitches in her knee, which she would be getting out later in the week, a decent black bruise on the side of her head, and the sling around her arm. She was thankful that she would look mostly healed for her first day back to classes.

She finished up in the bathroom and went into Jesse's room to make sure she had actually gone to sleep. Sean was already snoring loudly from his own room. Alex was only going to poke her head into the door of her sister's room, but when she got there she found herself stepping all the way into the room. All Alex had thought about since the attack was: *What if they had come for Jesse?* Alex knew the worst things to think about after a major trauma were the "What ifs," but she couldn't stop herself. Her sister was the only important thing she had left in this world. If anything ever happened to Jesse, Alex knew it would kill her too. She thought back to the day when their Uncle Jimmy died and how she ran away to the cliff. She had contemplated jumping off the edge and the only thing that had stopped her was Jesse. She knew that if Jesse was ever gone then there would be nothing left to keep her feet on solid ground.

Careful not to wake her sister up, Alex left the room and went into her own. The anticipation of seeing her friends and spending a day out of the house kept Alex awake. She took out the latest novel she was reading and tried to focus as she read the next two chapters. The story was about a boy and girl who had grown up together and who were eventually going to fall in love. The story made Alex's mind wander back to Jason and the meeting that took place after the cookout. Two days had passed since then, but the anger she felt towards Jason was still fresh.

Alex had always secretly wished that she could become a member of the Fu Lions. She had wanted to be the first woman voted into the club ever since she had talked to her father about it when she was young. The only other person she ever told about her wish was Jason when they were at the cliff one day. They had been talking about the club while sitting on their favorite rock, when she admitted the truth. She was afraid he would laugh at her, but he never did. He thought about it and declared it was a brilliant idea. They could be in the club together and "fight crime side by side." They were young teenagers then.

Relieved that Jason was sharing in her excitement she told him "I just have to find a way to convince them to vote me in."

"We have plenty of time to come up with a plan."

"They'll vote you in first, long before they even consider me."

"Then I'll have to convince them from the inside."

"You'll do that? For me?"

"Absolutely! They can't split the two of us up. We're better as a team."

"You promise?"

"I promise. We'll both be members one day."

He was right about them being a good team; they had always been better off together than apart. And he was right about them both becoming members one day, except now she was going to have to do it without his support. She hated being mad at him, she couldn't even remember having a fight with him that had lasted this long, but she decided that she needed at least a few more days before she could forgive him.

Alex's first day back to class was exactly how she expected it to be. The friends and classmates who hadn't seen her since the incident were horrified by how banged up she looked. Everyone else thought that she looked much better than before and were glad to see how quickly she was recovering. She had to answer the same questions over and over again; people wanted to hear the full story. Thankfully Kip was with her and between him, Wendy, and Ana, people left her alone for the most part. She hadn't actually been absent from any of her classes, but her Professors all gave her extensions on her homework assignments and offered her extra tutoring sessions if she needed them. She turned down the tutoring sessions, but happily accepted the homework extensions. She had completed most of her homework already but it never hurt to have a few extra days.

The three girls sat in their usual spot in the student center to eat their early lunch. Kip squeezed an extra chair around their table so that he could join them. Since this was the local community college mostly everyone knew about the club and Alex's association with it. That didn't stop people from giving Kip funny looks as he would plop down in the desk next to her in class and escort her all over campus. He gave her as much space as he could, but his shadow still always loomed over her and her friends. In Alex's third class the Professor refused to allow Kip into the room. He argued, but eventually was forced to sit in chair outside the door. When he left the Professor shut the door and winked to Alex. The Professor was one of Alex's favorites and vice versa. She knew Alex probably wanted a break from Kip and Alex was grateful to her.

"Ok," Wendy started as the class got into groups for an assignment. "What is the deal with the body guard?"

"He's not my body guard. He's just hanging out to make sure I'm safe."

"Right. A body guard."

Alex rolled her eyes, "Fine he's my body

guard. The club is worried that I might still be in danger."

Wendy peered around the room to make sure no one was listening, "Do you know who attacked you yet?"

Alex shook her head, "We're still waiting for the DNA results."

"Is the club going to go after the Reapers soon?"

"Why are you worried about it Wendy?"

"Hey, I grew up in this town too. I know the stories. The Lions were a small group of townsmen who managed to chase away a large group of weapons and drug dealers. It's almost like a fairytale you know. But what I do know is that the Reapers are stronger than you guys and if the Lions make a mistake the whole town will end up paying for it. The Reapers will come into town and take over and they will bring their drugs and guns with them. That will be bad for everyone. Besides that Sean is a Lion now and I don't want him to get hurt."

"I know, which is why I convinced the club to

wait before they tried to get back at the Reapers. I really can't tell you everything. I don't even know all the details myself, but I can tell you that the Lions are making a plan to get back at the Reapers and they're going to do it carefully. Since when do you care about Sean?

"Since he called and apologized this morning. So you're going to have a body guard for a while then?"

"I guess so. The club's set up a rotation of who's going to be with me and Jess for the next two weeks, for now."

"Is Jason going to be guarding you any time soon?"

"Nice try. Actually he's not on the schedule. We had an argument after the cookout in front of everyone. We haven't spoken since."

Wendy raised her eyebrow, "Oh? Do tell."

Alex described the meeting and the argument she had with Jason to Wendy while they pretended to work on their class assignment. Wendy was quick to agree that Jason was out of line, but also told Alex to not be so hard on him; he was only trying to protect her.

"I don't need to be protected."

"Last time I checked, you had a major head injury, stitches in your knee, your shoulder in a sling, and a "body guard" assigned to be with you 24/7."

"That's beside the point."

"No it's not. Your injuries are too fresh for the guys to forget. Think about how Jason must have felt when he found you. I know you keep denying that he likes you, but your still his best friend. How would you have felt if you found him like that? Would you turn around two days later and make him a part of something that could put him in that kind of danger again?"

"No, I guess not."

"Then give him a break. He might change his mind later along with some of the others. They all just need some time. Right now all they want is revenge."

Class ended. Wendy gave Alex a hug before they left the room, telling her she was glad she was ok. Kip had fallen asleep on the chair outside the class door and was getting laughed at by some of the other students. Alex rolled her eyes and kicked his chair, causing him to wake with a start.

"Aren't you supposed to be on alert for trouble?"

"I am. I only nodded off for a second."

"You have drool on your face." Kip wiped his mouth with the back of his hand and stood up. "Come on, let's go. I have lessons to teach today."

"Um, actually you don't have any lessons...for the whole week."

"What are you talking about?"

"The studio is still a crime scene, so you can't go in. Besides the place is a mess and you don't have a piano."

Alex sighed, "I forgot about the piano. I need to call and cancel my lessons then."

"Already taken care of."

"What? How?"

"Ron had a copy of your schedule in his office, with all your student's numbers. He went ahead and canceled your lessons for this week before our meeting the other night."

"Well, now what? I wasn't expecting to be done so early. I don't have any plans for the afternoon."

"We can do whatever you want. You'll have more time to do your homework now."

"Home then?"

"Sounds good to me."

"I'll bet. You couldn't possibly have slept good in that chair," Alex smiled.

"Ha, Ha. Very funny. I could use a nap now that you mention it."

Alex drove them home, where Kip took a nap on the couch and Alex completed all of her homework. Time passed slowly for Alex for the next two weeks. Most days were the same: Sean would spend the day with Jesse, Kip would go to school with Alex they would all eat dinner together, and then Sean would stay the night with the girls. Two whole weeks of being followed and watched constantly. On the weekend Jesse stayed with Carla and Russell and

Alex worked at the bar. Alex stayed with Sara and Ron for a whole weekend to give Sean a break and a chance to go home. Two whole weeks and nothing happened. The DNA results still had not come back from the lab and the club had not heard a single word from the Reapers. Alex had managed to keep the club from retaliating, but they were getting antsy again.

Kip took Alex to the doctor after the first week to get the stitches removed from her knee. It pinched as the doctor pulled them out, but Alex was relieved to find that the wound was no longer itchy once they were out. She was looking much better. She was finally allowed to release her arm from the sling and the bruise on her head was a much lighter color. She was feeling great and had heard that the club might remove her protection detail soon since things seemed to have quieted down.

Nate didn't show up to class again until the end of Alex's second week of being guarded. Since she hadn't heard from him in two weeks she decided to call him. He didn't answer the phone and despite leaving at least three messages he didn't respond. She had almost completely forgotten about him and was surprised when he showed up for class. He didn't approach her until later in the afternoon. Kip had become more lenient on his guard duties and was waiting for Alex in the car. Nate caught up to her after class and walked with her to the parking lot.

"Hey Alex, how've you been? I heard what happened a couple weeks ago. How are you doing?"

"I'm fine. Where have you been?"

"I had to go out of town for a while. I had a small family emergency to take care of."

"I hope everything is ok."

"Yup, everything's fine."

"I tried calling you a couple of times. I left like three messages."

"Yea sorry about that, my battery died. I had to leave town so fast that I accidentally left my phone charger at home. Anyway I actually wanted to ask you something."

"What's that?"

"Well, it's been a while since I've seen you

and I miss you. I was wondering if you might want to go to dinner with me again, maybe this weekend, you know, to catch up. Maybe Saturday night."

"Oh. I kind of have to work Saturday. I promised Dennis I'd help at the bar."

"Never mind then. It was worth a shot."

"Why don't you stop by the bar? Dennis usually gives me long breaks if we're not busy, and if we are you can hang out at the bar and talk to me while I work."

"Ok, cool. I'll see you Saturday then."

"See ya." Alex turned to walk away and as she did her laptop bag swung and hit Nate hard on the side of his leg. Nate cringed in pain. "I'm so sorry Nate. Are you ok?"

"Yea, I hit my leg on a table this weekend and it's bruised pretty bad that's all. I'll see ya."

Chapter 8

Friday morning the doorbell at the house rang. Sean and Jesse were already up and getting ready for the day. Alex was still asleep. She crawled out of bed and stepped into the hallway in time to see Sean letting Jason in. She quickly stepped back into her room and shut the door. Alex and Jason hadn't spoken still since their argument and Alex wasn't sure she was ready to see him. She was still mad at him for everything that had happened, but she knew that she would have to forgive him eventually. She ran a brush through her hair and walked out of her room.

"What are you doing here?" She asked him.

"Kip was busy today and asked me to take his place."

"He didn't mention anything yesterday."

"It was a last minute job for the club."

"Well, you can take Jess to school then, and Sean can stay here with me."

"I can't Alex," Sean said. "I promised Jess that since it was Friday I would take her and Rita and

Valerie to the movies after school."

"You're going to take three, thirteen-year-old girls to the movies?"

"Yea and I already ran it by Carla and Russell so I have to go."

"Fine." She turned to Jason, "I don't have any plans for today so you're stuck here."

"Actually I have plans today, so you'll be going with me."

"Well, we'll see you two later," Sean said. He and Jesse ran out of the house as fast as they could before they were caught between another argument between Jason and Alex.

"Where are we going?" She asked him.

"I towed a couple of Sportsters over in the trailer. I thought we could go for a ride."

"It's going to take a lot more than a motorcycle ride for me to forgive you, Jason."

"I know, but I was hoping it would be a start. Give me a chance will ya?"

"Fine. Where are we riding to?"

"It's a surprise woman, just go get ready."

Jason made himself comfortable on the couch while he waited for Alex to get herself dressed. She took her sweet time getting ready, picking out the right outfit and blow drying her hair, something she very rarely did. She was trying to make this as hard as possible for Jason as she could. She knew that eventually she would have to forgive him and get over it, but she was determined to make him pay for what he did to her. She came out of her bedroom in a pair of jeans, sneakers, and a t-shirt under her black leather jacket.

"Alright, I'm ready."

"Finally."

"Don't push it."

Jason led the way out of the house. There were two motorcycles in the driveway next to the Murphy Automotive truck, one red and one blue, fully equipped with helmets.

"I thought you only rode a Bad Boy," Alex smirked pleased with her comment.

"You know, it sounds so wrong when you say it like that. Leo's been working on these and needs someone to test drive them."

"Fine. I want the red one then," Alex said.

Alex put the house key in her jeans pocket and climbed onto the red bike before Jason could protest. She had to admit it felt really good to be on the back of a motorcycle again. It had been months since she'd really ridden. She revved the engine and nodded that she was ready to Jason. He led the way out of the driveway and down her small street.

Alex had never owned her own motorcycle. Her father used to let her ride on the back of his, but she was too young then to learn how to ride on her own. It was her Uncle Jimmy who taught her how to ride. He would take her out on his own motorcycle in the afternoons when school was over. They practiced in parking lots and on the back roads until she was good enough to drive on the main roads. When she turned 17 he took her to the DMV and she received her motorcycle driver's license. Alex continued to ride on her Uncle's bike after he passed away, but the bike was old and eventually it would no longer run. She kept the bike in the garage, but hadn't gotten around to having Leo fix it up for her yet.

She had no idea where Jason was going, but she was enjoying the ride so much that she stopped caring about where they would stop and wished they could ride like this forever. That morning when Jason came in the house she was determined to be angry at him for the rest of the day unless he came up with a really good apology, but the longer they rode together the less angry she became. They rode side by side down the narrow, winding back roads into town.

She noticed that Jason had gone the long way on purpose, taking them first away from the town and then back into town. They had been riding for 45 minutes before they reached the first traffic light of their small town. The light was red. They stopped next to each other.

Jason lifted the visor to his helmet, "Wanna race?"

"Where to?"

"The cliff."

"You're on."

Jason slid his visor back down and teasingly

revved his engine. She answered him back by revving her own engine. They each focused their energy on the light waiting for it to change to green. This was not their first time racing through the town. The first traffic light was positioned at the beginning of the town's main road which stretched from one end of town to the other. It would only take five minutes for them to race through the town and about ten more before they would reach the cliff. The trick to racing through town was not how fast they were able to drive, but how good they were at maneuvering through the traffic. The main road was only two lanes wide on their side and usually packed with cars and pedestrians. There were four more traffic lights to go through and then they would reach the end of town and head out onto some of the wider country roads.

The light turned green. Alex opened the throttle giving the bike everything it had, the tires screeching as she pulled away ahead of Jason. She knew the easiest way to beat him was to make it impossible for him to pass her and to force him to stop at a red light. That was her plan anyway. She was ahead, but not by much, as they reached the next stop light. She stopped behind a blue Prius, making Jason stop in the lane next to her, behind a pick-up truck.

Jason lifted his visor again, "I know what you're trying to do. It's not gonna work, Al."

"We'll see," she muttered to herself under her helmet. The second light turned green, the Prius was slower than the pick-up truck giving Jason an edge. He was a couple of car lengths ahead of her before he was forced to brake for another red light. She pulled up beside him and switched her focus onto the light and the traffic around them. There was only one light left in town, it was now or never for Alex to make a move. When the light turned green she quickly slid her motorcycle between the Prius and the pick-up. Riding between the two cars forced Jason to stay behind her. She inched the bike up to the front end of the Prius as they got closer to the last traffic light. The light was yellow and Alex sped through the light as it turned red. Jason was right behind her still between the two cars, but wasn't fast enough to make it through the light before it turned red. The truck driver was glaring at him through his window. The woman driving the Prius hadn't even noticed Alex and Jason as they were racing next to her.

Alex looked over her shoulder to make sure Jason wasn't still behind her. The light would only keep him there for 45 seconds and she tried to make the seconds last by continuing to speed down the road. The race wouldn't be over until one of them reached the trail opening leading to the cliff, which was still about ten minutes away from where Alex was. It didn't really feel like a win since she was speeding down the road alone. She slowed the bike down to give Jason a chance to catch up, hoping to make their race a bit more interesting.

She felt his presence long before she heard the sound of his engine approach from behind. She slowly began to give the bike more throttle so that she could keep her lead. He was right beside her. They raced side by side matching each other's pace the rest of the way to the trail. They both pulled over at the same time when they reached the trail.

"I win." Alex said.

"How do you figure that?"

"I pulled out of town first."

"The race was to here. It's a tie."

"Yea, but I let you catch up to me."

"What?"

"I didn't want to see you cry after losing, so I let you catch up to me."

"I don't think so. It takes skill to ride the way I do."

"Not much."

"I want a re-match on the way back."

"Fine."

Alex led the way down the trail. The hike was a little over half a mile long to get to the cliff. It was a narrow trail, covered in tree roots and small rocks that could easily make a person trip and fall. Technically this trail was a part of a nature park that had several hiking and biking trails for tourists or those who liked to hike, but this one was hidden by bushes. Not very many people actually noticed the trail when they were driving by and they would continue on to the main parking lot to pick a different trail. Neither Alex nor Jason had ever come across anyone on their secret trail and they preferred it that way. Finding it had been a complete accident when one day they were riding their bicycles by and Alex spotted a parting in the bushes. Alex and Jason had always liked to explore and go hiking on the different nature trails and neither of them had ever seen this one. They had parked their bikes behind the bushes and wandered down the trail to the cliff edge which became their favorite place to go.

Alex hadn't been to the cliff in a couple of months. She hadn't had a lot of time lately, but she was constantly wishing she could find the time to go. She could feel the wind blowing from the direction of the cliff as she pushed aside a tree limb. She was almost there and could smell the salt from the ocean and hear the waves crashing against the rocks below. They walked together in silence, Alex leading the way and Jason following behind carrying a backpack that was completely full to the top. Alex hadn't noticed the backpack earlier and had no idea what Jason brought with him, but she didn't bother to ask, the closeness of her favorite spot distracting her.

She broke through the trees, a gust of wind whipping her hair back from her face. She practically ran to the edge of the cliff, excited to finally be back. She stood as close to the edge as she dared and watched as the waves crashed against the bottom of the cliff face. She closed her eyes and breathed in the smell of the salty water. Jason wasn't beside her. She wondered where he wandered off to, but she wasn't willing to leave her spot to go look for him yet. She stood there for several minutes, feeling relaxed and free for the first time in weeks. Jason joined her at the edge and she reopened her eyes.

"Hungry?" he asked her.

"Um, yeah."

"I brought some food. Come on." He led her over to their favorite boulder and climbed his way to the top. She followed him up and when she got to the very top she was surprised to find that Jason had set up a picnic for them. There was a big red blanket spread out on the top of the boulder and on it were sandwiches, chips, and two cans of coke. Alex sat down next to Jason and he passed her a sandwich. It was an Italian sub from Subway. That made sense, she thought, Jason would never have actually made lunch himself, but she was glad that he had brought something with them. Jason finished his food long before Alex and he leaned back onto his elbows and watched her finish eating.

"What are you staring at?" She asked him. "You're kind of freaking me out."

"Sorry, I was just thinking."

"About?"

He shook his head, "Finish eating, then we'll talk."

The comment seemed strange to Alex, but the more she thought about it she realized that every important conversation the two of them ever had always happened here on this rock. Jason must have something important that he wanted to tell her. She ate the last bite of her sub and wrapped all of the trash back up into the small bag it came in.

"Ok, I'm finished. Talk."

Jason stood back up and turned his face toward the ocean. He always felt like he was on the top of the world when he stood here. Alex stayed where she was and waited for him to speak.

"These last two weeks have been rough," he said. "I couldn't figure out why they were so bad. Things just kept going wrong. Little things, like I locked my keys in the apartment at the clubhouse, or I forgot to fill the bike up with gas and I got stuck on the side of the road and had to push the bike all the way across town to get to the gas station. I even fell flat on my face in front of all the guys at our last meeting."

"Why are you telling me all of this?"

"Because, when I stood back up after falling Bobbie just looked at me and shook his head. He said I kept doing all these stupid things because I was distracted. I told him he was crazy and thought what could possibly be distracting me this much? But then I realized, I was distracted. The only thing I've been thinking about for the last two weeks has been you."

"What?"

"I know weird right. I tried to think of a time when we'd gotten into a fight this bad or when we'd been apart for this long and couldn't think of any."

"It's true, I've been thinking about it too. We've never fought like this before, but you've never hurt me like this before either."

"I know you're mad at me. You have every right to be. I really am sorry, Alex. I know I took it too far, but at the time I couldn't envision myself putting you into that kind of danger again."

"I know. I understand why you said no. I don't like it and I am still mad, but I understand."

"I'm sorry."

"I know you are." She paused. "There's something else isn't there?" He nodded. "I know that too. It's always been there, but lately I've been noticing it more, between the girls teasing me and the guys teasing you. Maybe they're seeing something that we never did."

"I see it now."

"Me too." They were quiet for several

minutes.

"Alex I have something else that I need to tell you." She waited for him to continue. "Wade finally made contact last night."

"What?"

"He called Dad, told him that it didn't matter how much we guarded you they would still find a way to get to you."

"What about Jesse?"

"He didn't mention her. Dad's assuming that she's safe, but he's going to let Sean and Kip continue watching you two"

"What happens now?"

"We need to find out who's giving them their information. Obviously you were right and someone from town has been talking to them. How else would they know that we've been keeping you guarded? Dad still wants you to come to the bar tomorrow night for work. The club is only going to let certain people into the bar and they're going to spread some false rumor about you and Jesse. Say that you're going out of town or something like that. We're gonna try to flush out our little rat."

"You think it will work?"

"We'll see."

"Ana and Wendy are supposed to be coming."

"That's fine. Let them come, they can help spread whatever rumor we decide to start."

"I invited Nate too."

"Good. I'm glad."

Alex scrunched up her nose in a quizzical look, "Why? Oh come on Jason you don't think he's the rat. What is it with you and him."

"I don't like him."

"That much is obvious."

They stayed on the boulder over the cliff for another little while, enjoying the quiet and peace that came from being there. Alex had a lot to think about now: this thing with Jason and Nate, her sister's safety, the fact that someone close to her was betraying her. She couldn't imagine that anyone she knew would betray her like this, and yet someone had. Who could it be? She thought.

Jason stood up abruptly, "Time to go," he

said.

"Why?"

"I have one more place to take you to today." He started cleaning up their lunch and repacking everything into his backpack. Alex stood up and helped him, then they walked back down the trail to their bikes.

"Where are we going now?"

"You'll see."

He pulled away and she followed right behind him all the way back into town and then straight to her studio.

"What are we doing here?" she asked. He didn't answer, just kept walking towards her studio door and unlocked it. He indicated that she should go inside ahead of him. When she walked through the door the studio had been transformed. The walls were repainted, the furniture put back in its place, damaged pictures and mirrors replaced. The place looked amazing, even better than it did before. No trace of the attack had been left behind.

"How did you..." He shook his head and

pointed toward the lesson room. The door was shut. She walked up to it and found it unlocked. She looked to Jason, who nodded, before opening the door. As soon as the door was open she was greeted with a loud "Surprise!" All of the club members were packed into the small room waiting for her to arrive. The entire room was redone as well and looked beautiful.

"The guys have been working on it all week," Jason said from behind her.

"This place looks amazing you guys, I can't believe you did all this."

"And now for the piece de resistance..." Bobbie said with a bad French accent. The men all shifted to the sides of the room, making a clear path to where the piano had been. In its place was a brand new, shiny, black, baby grand piano.

"Where did you get that?"

"Jason did some research and found it. Then we all chipped in to get it for you. All of this was Jason though."

"Thank you," was all she could manage to

whisper as she turned to face Jason.

Chapter 9

The bar opened as planned on Saturday night with only the club and their invited guests. Jesse was going to spend yet another night at Carla's with the girls. When all this is over, Alex thought, Jesse needs to start spending more time at home. For the time being though, Alex was thankful that Jesse had somewhere to go, somewhere safe. Alex was starting to have her own doubts about her dream of joining the club. Jesse wouldn't be any safer, but she might end up being in more danger. Jesse might also be required to spend even more nights out of the house because Alex would be home less often. These were things that Alex would have to start considering before she approached the club again.

Despite limiting the customers, the bar was completely packed with people from town. Alex took up her position behind the bar with Dennis and started serving drinks. It was hard for Alex to imagine any one of the people in the bar betraying her, yet one of them had. She hoped tonight they could find out who it was and put an end to the war between the Lions and the Reapers.

The music was loud as Alex served drinks to the customers. She looked up from the bar and gave a little wave to Wendy who was standing across the room with Sean and Ana. Alex knew Sean and Wendy would find their way to each other, she laughed to herself. Jason walked over to them and nodded to Alex as he walked past. He whispered something to each of them, then the four of them separated and made their way around the bar talking to as many people as they could reach. Alex realized that they were spreading their rumor. She found herself wondering what the club decided to say about her and her sister. Whatever it was it had to be good enough to convince the rat to tell the Reapers.

Alex looked up in time to see Nate walking through the door and watched as he scanned the crowd looking for her. He waved and pushed his way through the crowd to get to where she was. Wendy was across the room when she noticed Nate walking in and she quickly tried to beat him over to the bar.

"Hey Alex," he said arriving before Wendy and taking a seat at the bar directly in front of Alex.

"Alex!!" Wendy jumped in stealing her attention away from Nate. "I just heard the news." Alex gave Wendy a strange look.

"What news?" Nate asked.

Wendy ignored him, "I can't believe you didn't tell me you were leaving town," she winked.

"Oh, I'm sorry Wendy it happened so fast that I haven't had a minute to tell you yet," Alex said playing her part.

"You're leaving town?" Nate asked.

"She's going to move in with a cousin of hers from out of state," Wendy interrupted again.

"I didn't know you had other family."

"Neither did I," Alex said giving Wendy a pointed look. "Like I said everything has happened so fast, but I got a phone call the other day from a distant cousin of mine who found out about everything that's been happening here and she's offered to let me and Jess stay with her for a while until things cool down."

"I thought things were getting better now," Nate said.

"They are, I just think that a break will be a good thing for Jess. I have to think about what will be best for her in the future and I've been wondering if getting out of this town might be the best option."

"I'm gonna miss you so much," Wendy said. She was trying to keep Alex's attention away from Nate, something Jason told her to do, and Alex knew it.

"Hey by the way Wendy I just saw you and Seany together, how's that going?"

"What? Nothing's going on."

"That's not what I asked. He's staring at you."

"What? Really? Do I look ok tonight?"

Alex shook her head, "You look great Wendy, just go over there and talk to him would ya?" Wendy eyed Nate one more time and then left the two of them together at the bar.

"What was that about?" Nate asked.

"What do you mean?"

"She was trying to keep me away from you."

"Oh, no she wasn't. She was just mad at me for not telling her about me and Jess going out of town."

"What about the Sean thing?"

"Sean and Wendy dated for a little while when we were in high school. Sean and Jason were a year ahead of me and Wendy in high school and when we got there the boys watched out for us. We all grew up together anyway, but in high school something changed between Wendy and Sean and they started to date. By the time Sean graduated the two of them were crazy over each other and the rest of us were convinced they'd get married."

"What happened that they didn't?"

"Sean has a sister our age named Elise. Elise decided she'd move up into the city where they had an Aunt and Uncle. Their parents begged Sean to go with her to keep her out of trouble, so he did. He left without asking Wendy to wait for him. It was a mess, they were both heartbroken."

"But he came back."

Alex nodded, "Elise and Sean got into a little

trouble up in the city. Sean ended up coming home and Elise is married and traveling the world with her new husband."

"Everything worked out just fine."

"Almost." Alex looked over to where Sean was standing next to Wendy, "They'll figure it out soon enough." Jason was standing with them. He nodded to Alex and joined the conversation around him.

"So you're leaving." It was more of a statement than a question.

"When?"

"I'm not sure yet exactly. As soon as possible I suppose."

"That's a shame. I really wanted the chance to ask you out again."

"Oh. Nate I don't think we should see each other right now since I'm leaving town."

"Alright, I understand."

"I'm sorry Nate, I..."

"It's fine, Alex, don't worry about it. Can I get a beer?"

"Sure." Alex pulled a glass out from under the counter and poured Nate a beer from the tap. "Guinness, ok? It's my favorite."

"Sounds good."

Alex slid him the beer then turned and helped the next few customers. She and Dennis worked hard for an hour before the rush finally calmed down.

"Go take a break Alex I can handle the rest," Dennis said to her.

"Are you sure?"

"I'm fine. I'll shout if I need you."

"Alright." She poured herself a Guinness, stepped out from behind the bar, and took the open stool next to Nate who was texting a message on his phone.

"Hang on a sec," he said as she sat next to him. He finished typing the text and said, "Sorry about that. I've been trying to catch up on all my messages and stuff from my trip. Man, I missed this phone, I can't believe I left it at home."

"I thought you said you left the charger at home and the battery died."

"Right."

They talked for several minutes as the music played on and people continued to talk and dance. The music switched to a slow song; Put Your Lights On by Santana and Everlast, one of her favorite songs. Nate continued to talk to her about nothing in particular. She tuned him out and focused on the music, closing her eyes as she listened. She couldn't shake the feeling that someone was watching her; she opened her eyes and caught Jason staring at her from across the room. Unlike at the cookout a couple of weeks ago, he held her gaze as he took a swig of his beer. He placed the empty beer bottle down on the table where Sean and Wendy were sitting away from the crowd. Jason motioned for her to join him on the dance floor.

"Would you excuse me for a minute, Nate?"

"Um, yeah I guess." Alex finished the last of her beer and climbed down from the tall stool. She slowly made her way towards Jason who was now standing in the middle of the crowd on the dance floor. He held out his hand to her, she took it. The world around them disappeared as Jason led her across the small dance floor. Sean led Wendy to the dance floor to join them. It didn't take long for the rest of the dancers to realize this was a private dance between the two couples. The other dancers stopped and cleared the dance floor, the customers from the bar made a circle around the two couples. Everyone watched as Jason, Alex, Sean, and Wendy danced without noticing anything around them.

Alex didn't notice that Nate was watching from where she left him in the bar still drinking his beer as he eyed them. She didn't notice when he slammed his money for the beer on the counter and she didn't notice when he stood up and walked out of the building, glancing back at her before he shut the door behind him and disappeared.

Chapter 10

Three hours later, at 1:00 in the morning, Alex lay in her bed at home staring at the ceiling. She couldn't sleep, all she could think about was her dance with Jason. It was the first time she noticed the way he looked at her. The first time she looked at him the same way. No matter how much she tossed and turned she couldn't lose the image of his face, the feel of his hand in hers and his other hand pressing into her back.

She couldn't stand it any longer. She got out of bed and went into the kitchen to get a drink. She filled a glass with water from the sink faucet. The water tasted stale in her mouth from the beers she had earlier. She poured it out and went into the bathroom to brush her teeth. Jess had been the last to brush her teeth and left the toothpaste on the counter without its top. Alex rolled her eyes at the mess Jesse had left on the edge of the sink. She brushed her teeth quickly and then cleaned up the mess. She caught site of herself in the mirror. She looked completely different than she had two weeks ago after the attack. She was mostly healed save for a small hint of a bruise still on the side of her face. All of the pain was gone; she was finally back to normal. Tonight was one of the first nights that Sean didn't stay over. Alex was actually supposed to have gone home with Wendy, but she had changed her mind after her dance with Jason. When the music had stopped Alex realized that what she thought was an intimate private moment between her and Jason was being watched by everyone in the bar, which meant that everyone in the club and everyone in town had see them together. It shouldn't have been a big deal. The two of them had danced together in the bar before, but this time was much different and now everyone knew it.

She went back into her bedroom. Sleep was not going to come to her tonight, not if she kept thinking about Jason. Before she even knew what she was doing, Alex slipped on a pair of jean shorts and a t-shirt, grabbed her purse and keys, and left the house. She didn't know where she wanted to go, but she couldn't stay in the house anymore; it was too quiet and lonely in there without Jesse and Sean. She got into her car and started to drive through the town. The town was dark and silent, most people were asleep in their beds. There was an unseasonable chill in the air as she drove with her windows cracked open. She was driving to make herself tired enough to sleep when she got back, but she never went home. Instead she drove to the clubhouse. She had a key to the clubhouse on her key ring. She unlocked the door and went inside. All of the lights were off in the bar. Dennis must have gone home without cleaning because the place was a mess. There was broken glass on the floor from someone who dropped a half-empty bottle of beer and the chairs, tables and stools weren't lined up like they usually were.

Alex walked passed all of the mess and headed to the back hallway where the display of her father's bike was. Normally she would've stopped, but tonight she walked straight passed it and turned right up the back stairway to the apartment where Jason was staying. She only had to knock twice for him to answer.

"Can I come in?" She asked him. He said nothing, just moved his body so that she could pass by him into the apartment. "I'm sorry, I know it's late, but I couldn't sleep."

"It's alright, I couldn't either." She sat down on the small sofa that was in the middle of the room between the bed and the kitchen. "Want a beer?" He asked her. She nodded and he pulled one out from the fridge. He handed it to her and sat down next to her on the couch their legs close, but not touching. She took a sip of the beer and stood. She walked into the kitchen area across from where she left Jason on the couch and stood behind the island counter in the middle of the kitchen so that she was facing him.

"Is something wrong?" He asked her.

"No, I just feel restless. Like I can't sit still tonight."

"Why?"

"I'm not exactly sure. All I can think about is what you said on the cliff and about the dance earlier."

He nodded, "I know. I feel the same." He

stood and walked over to the island counter and leaned his body on the opposite side as her.

"What are we going to do about it?"

Jason stood up straight and finished the last mouthful of his beer. He put the bottle down on the counter and crossed over to the side where Alex was standing. That was when he kissed her. For the first time in the 22 years of him knowing her Jason did what he'd wanted to do since they were young teenagers. He wrapped his arms around her and kissed her, and to his relief she kissed him back.

Downstairs the bar was still dark, still silent, and still a mess.

The Informant left the bar early that night to make his report to the Reapers. He had discovered some new information about the Murphy girls and knew that the Reapers would want to hear it as soon as possible. He texted them from the bar to tell them he was on his way and then he left while everyone's attention was on the dance floor. He rode his motorcycle down the dark, deserted streets of the small town. It took him twenty minutes to reach the little log cabin in the woods. The truth was, the cabin really freaked him out and he hated to go there. Wade was hiding in the cabin; he said it was the only place he could go where the Lions would never find him. He had gone into hiding the moment the Reapers had made their assault on Alex and had been at the cabin ever since

The Informant stopped his motorcycle in front of the cabin on the gravel driveway, next to the other motorcycles. There were several motorcycles parked in the driveway, but the 1998 Harley Davidson Fat boy in all black could only belong to Wade. The Informant put the kickstand down on his bike and removed his helmet. As he walked to the cabin's front door, the informant passed by the unmistakable Reaper on the end of the exhaust pipe of Wade's motorcycle, who's eyes would light up whenever Wade revved his motorcycle engine. There were two men guarding the front door, each one heavily armed. They were expecting him. The first one checked his body for weapons and the second went inside to inform Wade of his arrival. Once he had been checked thoroughly, the second came back outside and led him into the cabin.

Wade was sitting at a small table in the back room eating his dinner. A bright red lobster lay in the center of Wade's plate and butter was dripping from his face and fingers. The Informant would have laughed if he wasn't so afraid.

"You better have something good this time," Wade said with his mouth full.

"I do," the Informant replied.

"Well, let's hear it then." There were two more armed guards standing on each side of Wade. Wade motioned for the Informant to sit in the empty chair in front of his.

"I just came from the Lion's bar. They had an exclusive party tonight and I heard a rumor while I was there."

"A rumor? You'll have to do better than a rumor."

"It was confirmed by Alex herself and her best

friend. Apparently Alex and her sister plan on leaving town as soon as possible. Some distant cousin of theirs has made contact and they're going to go stay with them for a while."

"Cousin? She doesn't have any relatives."

"That's what I thought too, but Alex said that it was a distant cousin that she didn't know about." Wade wiped his face with a napkin and slowly stood up from the table. He walked around the table and sat down on the edge of it in front of the Informant, their faces only inches apart.

"I wasn't asking if she had relatives. I simply made the statement that she didn't have any, something I know for a fact since I killed all of her living family. Now are you telling me that I'm a liar?"

"No, no, no, no, that's not what I meant. Only, there must be someone that we didn't know about. Otherwise where would she be going? And why would she lie to everyone?"

Wade smiled an evil grin that was followed by a slow, deliberate laugh. He turned to his men and pointed a finger at the Informant as if to say "Can you believe what this guy just said?" The men joined their boss in his laughter. Wade stood up again and the Informant saw something silver flash in his hand: the tool used to crack the lobster claws. Wade walked around the chair his Informant was sitting in until he stood directly behind him. Wade snatched the Informant's hand and slipped the shell cracker around his middle finger and squeezed.

Wade leaned down and whispered into the Informant's ear, "Apparently you didn't hear me clearly the first time. I killed that girl's entire family. I shot her mother in front of her and shot her father in a bar. I injected her uncle with an untraceable drug that appeared to give him a heart attack. I know everything about the Murphy family and their little club, and I know for a fact that she has no family." Wade squeezed the claw crackers until he heard a loud crack and the Informant yelled out in pain as the bone in his middle finger snapped. Satisfied, Wade sat back down in his chair and resumed eating his dinner.

"Where is she going then?" The Informant asked, tears welling in his eyes.

"Obviously the Lions want us to believe that they're sending the girls away. It is a play in order to get us to attack sooner."

"What are we going to do?"

"We? You mean *you*. Several months ago, you came to me begging to become a Reaper and saying that you would do anything to become a member. You offered to go 'undercover' and find a weakness in the Lions. It was your own suggestion. You came up with an elaborate plan to kidnap the Murphy girl and I made the mistake of agreeing to it. You trashed her studio, but came back empty handed. You failed me. I'm giving you one more chance to prove yourself. Bring Alex to me or I'll kill you instead."

"But they'll be expecting me now."

"Figure it out. The clock is ticking. I suggest you get moving."

"Yes, sir." The Informant stood up from his chair and walked to the door, his finger throbbing.

"Oh, and Nate," Wade said, "don't ever correct me again."

Nate nodded and left the cabin.

Chapter 11

The sunlight streaming in from the window is what finally woke Alex up at 10:00 in the morning. She opened her eyes to the small upstairs apartment in the clubhouse. She shot straight up as she remembered what happened the night before. She looked over at Jason who was still asleep in the bed beside her. She had a headache and desperately wanted a cup of coffee. She quietly slipped out of the bed and put her shorts back on. The pockets were heavy with her cell phone and her pocket knife. She looked for her t-shirt, but couldn't find it amidst the mess in Jason's apartment. He really needs to clean up more often she thought to herself. She gave up and settled for the shirt he was wearing in the bar last night. It was a white, button up t-shirt that was obviously too big for her, but it felt comfortable and was good enough for now.

She walked into the kitchen to make coffee, but the coffee pot was nowhere in sight. She rummaged around in the few cabinets, but couldn't find it anywhere.

"What are you looking for?" She heard Jason's voice. He was sitting up in bed watching her go through all of his stuff.

"How long have you been awake?"

"Long enough to see you going through all my cabinets."

"I can't find the coffee pot."

"Ah. That would be downstairs in the bar."

"What's it doing down there?"

"The guys commandeered it from me at a meeting not too long ago. They like to have coffee during our meetings sometimes and the old coffee pot in the bar broke, so they stole mine."

"Why didn't you bring it back up afterwards?"

"I did, but they took it again at the next meeting. I've been meaning to get a new one for up here."

"Guess I'm going downstairs then. Would you like a cup?" She asked as she pulled the coffee out of the fridge and a mug from one of the upper cabinets.

"Coffee sounds great," he said and she

reached in and pulled out another coffee mug. "Hey come here." She left the kitchen and walked back over to the side of the bed where she had slept and sat back down next to him. He leaned up and kissed her, "Good morning."

"Good morning."

"Is that my shirt?"

"Yeah, I couldn't find mine. This place is a mess."

"I know. My shirt looks good on you, though." She threw the bed pillow at him and hit him in the face as she got up and went back into the kitchen.

"If I know you, you probably hid my shirt while I was sleeping last night, so I wouldn't be able to leave without you knowing it."

"Leave? The only place your going is downstairs to make me coffee."

"Oh? And then what?"

"Then you're coming back up here and staying for the rest of the day." She answered him by walking back over to the couch and throwing another pillow at his face. He laughed at her, "Hey put on some shoes before you go down there was glass all over the floor last night."

She looked down at her bare feet, "You're right, I remember seeing it before I came up." She found her shoes by the door and sat back down on the bed to put them on. "Alright I'll be right back." She grabbed the two mugs and the bag of coffee and left the apartment.

"Hurry up," he called after her as she left. He decided to go into the bathroom and brush his teeth and put on some clothes before she came back.

It didn't take long for Alex to find the coffee pot at the end of the bar. It was funny that she hadn't noticed it when she was working last night. She filled the pot with water and hit the "Brew" button on the machine. She decided to make a full pot of coffee even though there were only two of them. She heard glass crunching behind her and turned.

"Alex?" It was Wendy.

"Wendy? What are you doing here?"

"I think I should be asking you the same thing."

"Did you sleep here last night?"

Wendy nodded, "I was in the first room down the hall."

"Sean?"

Wendy nodded again, "Jason?" Alex nodded. Both girls smiled. "I hate to say I told you so."

"No you don't."

"No, I really don't," Wendy agreed

"I made enough coffee for 4. Want some?"

"Yes please. My head is pounding."

"Have a little too much to drink last night? Are you sure it's Sean in the other room?"

"Very funny, Alex." Alex found two more mugs under the bar for Wendy and Sean. The timer on the coffee pot beeped and Alex poured two mugs for Wendy and Sean.

"Here," she handed the mugs to Wendy.

"Thanks. Oh, that smells so good. Hey I'm gonna go get dressed, do you want to do something today."

"Sure, maybe the four of us can go to a movie or something later."

"That sounds great. I'll go tell Sean."

"I'll see you later then."

Alex poured herself a cup of coffee. She decided she wanted to drink some of hers now before she went back upstairs. Everything was going to be different now. She had some explaining to do to her sister when she picked her up later and to Nate when she saw him in school. Nate. She had totally forgotten about him until now. He must really hate her for what happened last night. She ditched him at the bar to go and dance with Jason, whom he considered his rival, with good cause, and then the dance turned into a spectacle for the whole town to watch. She hoped she didn't hurt him. She still liked Nate, just not in the way he wanted her too. She sighed. Nate.

Upstairs Jason was pulling a shirt on over his head when he heard his cell phone ring. The ringer was on loud so he could hear it, but it took him forever to find it. He gave a yelp as he stubbed his toe on the corner of the bed. He remembered that he had put his phone in the drawer next to his bed, the same drawer where he kept his gun and full magazine clip, like he did every night in case he needed to find it fast. By the time he located his cell phone the voicemail had picked up. He scrolled through his missed calls to see who it had been. Victor's number showed up on the screen. He immediately hit redial.

Nate. Alex sipped her coffee as she heard a loud thump and Jason yelling, "Ouch," from upstairs. She shook her head. Nate was still on her mind. He had been acting weird last night after she told him she was leaving town. It wasn't true and she hated having to lie to him, but obviously Jason told Wendy to make sure Nate heard their false rumor. Otherwise why would she have rushed over to tell him when he walked into the bar? Alex tried to recall some of the other weird things Nate had done in the past couple weeks. He hadn't been in town, but he ignored her calls and texts which wasn't like him. He lied about leaving his phone at home. Something was bothering Alex and she couldn't quite put her finger on what it was. Something about when he was turning to walk away from her. She remembered that she bumped his leg with her bag and it hurt him. His right leg. Her mind flashed back to the attack at the studio. She remembered that she had managed to stab her attacker in his leg. His right leg. She needed to talk to Jason, he had been right about Nate all along. As she turned away from the coffee pot *he* was standing there. She dropped the coffee mug on the floor.

"Hey Vic, you called?" Jason said when he heard Victor answer.

"Yeah, hey Jason. You asked me to call you first when the DNA results came in on that blood at the studio."

"And?"

"Well I got the results about an hour ago."

"Who was it?"

"The blood belonged to a male in his early

twenties."

"Do we know him?"

"Yes. Well, at least I know that Alex does."

"Who is it Vic?"

"Nate..." Jason didn't hear the rest of the name. All he heard was a loud crash and a girl's scream coming from downstairs.

Alex wasn't the one who screamed. When she dropped the coffee mug on the floor, the crash made Wendy come running out of the hallway bedroom. Wendy saw Nate holding a gun in his hand pointed at Alex, which is what made her scream. Nate obviously wasn't expecting Wendy to be there. Her scream was enough of a distraction for Alex to get out from the aim of the gun. She ducked down as he turned to look at Wendy and ran around him. She kicked him in his lower back, crumpling him to the floor. She knew there were several guns hidden in the clubhouse: one under the bar, two in the meeting room, and one under the display of her father's bike. The meeting room was the closest place to her and she made a dash for it, grabbing Wendy as she ran by. They made it into the meeting room, but Nate would be close behind soon.

"Are you okay, Alex?" Wendy asked.

"Fine. You?"

"I'm good. I'm sorry I screamed."

"It's okay. It gave me a chance to slip away. The boys must have heard you too. They're probably heading down the hall right now."

Alex locked the door and ran over to the long table that was centered in the middle of the room. She bent down and used her hands to feel the underside of the table until she found what she wanted. There were two gun holsters attached to the underside of the table with extra gun clips. She pulled down both guns, setting one on the table with the magazine, and loaded one for herself. Wendy, now beside her, quickly loaded the other one with skills that Alex had forgotten she had.

"What?" Wendy asked when she caught Alex smile at her. "I grew up here too you know."

Alex shook her head, "You ready for this?"

"As ready as I'll ever be."

The two girls waited on either side of the door. Nate was there now, trying to open the door first by pushing with his shoulder and then by kicking it with his foot. Alex had chosen this room for a reason: it was the most secure room in the clubhouse. The door was reinforced and almost impossible to break down. The next thing they heard was a gunshot, and the door handle fell on the floor.

Jason didn't recognize the scream; it didn't sound like Alex to him. He threw his phone down without even hanging it up and grabbed the gun and extra clip out of his drawer. He bolted down the stairs into the main bar area. He arrived in time to see Alex and Wendy running down the back hallway. Nate was beginning to recover from Alex's kick. Jason saw him get up and begin to run down the hallway after the girls, gun in hand. Instinct kicked in as Jason followed them into the back hallway. He could see Alex pulling Wendy into the meeting room and knew she would be going for the guns hidden there. Jason would have ran straight to her had he not heard another crashing noise in the room beside him. He looked into the doorway and saw a guy his age wrestling with Sean. Sean was fighting hard but the other guy had the advantage of surprise. Jason knew there must be more men outside and he knew he wouldn't get through this alone. He made the decision to help Sean first. He knew Alex and Wendy would be alright; they both knew how to shoot and there were two guns in that room. Alex knew what to do and would be fine...he hoped.

Jason burst into the room and took a shot at the guy fighting Sean. The shot gave Sean the help he needed to overpower the other guy. He punched him, knocking him out, and took his gun.

"The girls?" Sean asked.

"In the meeting room. Nate's outside the door."

"Alex went for the guns?" Jason nodded. "Smart girl."

"You ready?" Jason asked Sean.

"As ready as I'll ever be."

Before either of them was able to leave the room, they heard a gunshot and a series of loud crashes coming from the end of the hallway.

The doorknob fell on the floor. Alex nodded to Wendy to be ready. Wendy nodded back. They waited, but nothing happened. Nate didn't come through the door. Alex made a face and looked at Wendy.

"What's he waiting for?" Wendy asked in a whisper. Alex never got the chance to answer because as soon as Wendy finished her question both of the windows on the other side of the room were smashed. Two more men came in from each window. The girls ducked down to protect their faces from the flying glass giving the men a chance to crawl in without the girls firing at them. Amidst the confusion, Nate shoved the door open and made his way into the meeting room. The girls were outgunned, the men surrounding them on all sides. Wendy and Alex were forced to drop their weapons on the floor and raise their hands above their heads.

Alex knew they had come for her; she was afraid of what that meant for Wendy.

"Alright, I'll go with you," Alex said.

"Alex, don't."

"It's ok, Wendy, I'll be fine." She turned to Nate, "Let's go."

Nate grinned and motioned for her to walk out of the room in front of him. At that moment Jason appeared from behind and pushed Nate away from Alex.

"Get out of here, Alex," she heard Jason yell. Alex remained where she was not wanting to leave without him. This time it was Wendy who did the leading, pulling Alex out of the room by her arm. They were met by Sean in the hallway who told them to head out front and call for help. He ran into the room and disappeared. Wendy dragged Alex the rest of the way back to the room where she had spent the night. The room was upside down from the fight the boys had in there earlier. Everything was turned over and there was an unconscious man laying in the middle of the floor. Wendy dug through the mess and was able to locate her cell phone. She and Alex left the room and went back out into the bar. They would have called the police, but they were met by two more men in the bar. The girls were now unarmed and completely defenseless. The men grabbed both of them, holding their guns to their heads so that they were unable to fight back.

They half dragged, half carried Alex and Wendy out to the parking lot where there was a grey, windowless van parked. Nate and the two that broke into the meeting room were running into the parking lot from the back of the clubhouse. Sean and Jason were right behind them firing their guns. The man holding Alex turned his attention to the gunshots. He raised his gun and fired toward Jason forcing Jason to duck to avoid the bullets. Alex pushed the gun into the air and kneed the man in the stomach. He fell to the ground and dropped his gun.

Sean ran towards the man holding Wendy. Alex picked the gun up from the ground and aimed it at Wendy's attacker. The man was confused, not knowing who to shoot towards; he pointed his gun at

Alex, but never got a chance to fire. Sean ran into the man knocking all three of them to the ground. Alex ran over and helped Wendy stand up.

"Wendy run back to the bar, you have to call for help." Alex pushed Wendy towards the bar and turned back to help Sean. Jason was still fighting with Nate on the other side of the parking lot. Sean and the man were fighting each other on the ground. Alex made to step forward, but was pulled back by a man behind her. The driver from the van got out when he noticed the commotion, he grabbed Alex from behind not giving her the chance to help Sean. There were too many of them. It was six against four, the element of surprise on the side of the former. With one man down inside the clubhouse, Alex being held and Wendy calling for help the numbers were changed to five against two. The men gained the upper hand holding Jason and Sean at gunpoint. The fight was over and the men had Alex. They threw her into the back of the van. The driver got back in the front and Nate jumped into the back with Alex. The other three got onto the back of their motorcycles.

The last thing Alex saw before Nate shut the van's back door was Wendy kneeling beside Sean on the ground and Jason running towards the van.

"Sean, are you ok?" Wendy asked him frantically. She knelt down next to him and pressed her shirt against a gash on his forehead.

"Fine. Did you call the police?"

"Yes they're on their way." Jason ran to the front of the clubhouse where his bike was parked.

"Jason, what are you doing?" Sean asked.

"I'm going after her."

"Are you crazy? You can't. They have you outnumbered five to one."

"I'm not going to just let them get away. Wait here for the cops and call the guys. You need to check on the guy in your room and make sure he's still unconscious. Tie him up and hide him in the basement. I don't want the cops anywhere near him. If I don't come back with Alex, he's mine."

Jason started the bike and sped out of the parking lot after the van. They had a head start, but

Jason was a much faster driver and the van was too slow. In less than a minute he was able to catch up to them. They were driving down the windy back roads where there wasn't very much traffic at this time of the day. Jason got in as close as he could to the motorcycle in the back. He didn't really have a plan; he was making things up as he went. He reached over and squeezed the brakes on the handle of the other guy's bike, causing the man to jerk his bike away. The man crashed into the bike next to him, causing both of them to run off the road. Two down, Jason thought, only one more bike left.

The third motorcyclist saw what happened in his side mirror and was expecting Jason. He took his gun out and fired before Jason could get anywhere near him. Jason had to swerve to avoid the shots.

Inside the van, Nate sat holding his gun pointing at Alex. They both heard the gunshots coming from outside.

"What's going on?" Nate asked the driver.

"Two of the bikes are missing. I can't see anything."

The reason the driver couldn't see Jason or the third man was because they were both driving on opposite sides of the van in the van's blind spots. This gave Jason the time he needed to plan his next move. If he could only get rid of this third man somehow then he should be able to take on the other two in the van easily.

"Whatever happens, don't stop," Nate told the driver. The gun was still pointed at Alex, but Nate wasn't paying attention to her. She kicked out with her leg. Nate wasn't expecting it and the force of the kick on his broken finger made him drop his gun. Alex punched him in the face as hard as she could, breaking his nose. She ran to the back of the van and opened the door.

Jason was still trying to figure out what to do next when he saw the back door to the van open wide. The door smacked into the third motorcyclist and sent him flying off his bike. Jason braked enough so that he could see inside the van. He saw Alex standing in the doorway and Nate sitting in the back clutching a bleeding nose.

"Jason!" Alex yelled to him. Jason pulled the bike up as close as he could to the van.

"You're gonna have to jump!" He yelled to her.

"JUMP!? Are you crazy?"

Jason reached his hand out to her, "I'll catch you."

Alex was seriously contemplating the plan. In theory, if she reached out and took Jason's arm she might be able to lean over him enough to twist her leg over the bike that way she would only have to give a little jump to land on the back of his bike. Behind her Nate snapped back to reality. He saw Alex reaching out to take Jason's hand and thought his mind was playing tricks on him. Was she really that crazy? Nate couldn't let her get the best of him again. He stood and walked towards the back of the van and reached for Alex, intending to pull her backwards, but at the same time the driver hit a bump that forced Nate forward into Alex. Alex was flung from the van and slammed against the open back door. She grabbed onto the top of the door, managing to get a good enough grip to hang on. Her right foot found the door handle which gave her a better hold on the door. There was no way she was going to be able to jump from the van in this position. She clung on for dear life as Jason pulled up even closer.

She shook her head to him as he reached out to help her, "It's no use Jason. You need to get out of here."

"I'm not leaving you!"

"You have too," she shouted back. "I'll be ok, I know it."

"No Alex!"

Nate was standing in the doorway; he reached his hand out to help her back into the van. Alex knew she could trust him to help her, she knew that he had to bring her back alive.

She turned her head to Jason one last time and yelled, "Call Donnie!" Then she let go of the door with her left hand and took hold of Nate's arm. He pulled her backwards into the van, slamming the door shut behind them. Jason slowed his bike down and watched the van taking Alex away until he couldn't see it anymore. He had failed to bring her home this time, he would never be able to live with himself if something happened to her. He slowed his bike down to a stop and then he turned the bike back towards town.

Chapter 12

Victor and Ryan arrived at the clubhouse only seconds after Sean tied up the man in his room and locked him in the downstairs basement. They were the first on the scene; Victor had heard some of the commotion over Jason's cell phone and immediately got hold of Ryan and headed over to the clubhouse.

"What happened?" Ryan asked. Wendy was standing over Sean at one of the tables. Her shirt was covered in his blood and she was holding a towel against his forehead.

"Six men attacked the bar," she answered Ryan. "One of them was Nate."

Victor nodded, "I got the DNA results back on Alex's attacker. It was a match for Nate. I was on the phone with Jason when I heard him drop his phone. I heard a lot of noise and commotion. We came over as fast as we could."

"Me, Alex, Jason, and Sean all spent the night here after the party," Wendy began to explain. "When I got up this morning Alex was making coffee. I left her in the bar to bring a cup of coffee to Sean. Next thing I heard was a loud crash in the bar, so I went out to see what happened. I found Nate holding a gun to Alex and I screamed. The rest happened so fast. We ran to the meeting room, two more men came in through the windows, Nate caught up to us, Jason and Sean caused a distraction and we slipped away. We went out front and were ambushed again by two more men. There was a big fight outside and I got away and called 911. Sean got hit in the head and I can't stop the bleeding." Wendy's adrenaline was beginning to wear off. Her hands and legs were shaking. Sean took her hand and made her sit down. She put her face in her hands.

"Where are Alex and Jason?" Victor asked.

"They got Alex." Sean answered.

"What do you mean they got Alex?"

"I mean that they ambushed and outnumbered us and managed to get her into their van and drive away."

"What about Jason?"

"He went after her."

"What?!"

"He got on his bike and drove after them. I couldn't stop him."

An ambulance arrived two minutes behind Victor and Ryan, along with several more police cars. Five minutes later every member of the club was also on the scene. Wendy and Sean both gave their statements to the police and explained what happed to the Lions at the same time. The EMTs in the ambulance cleaned up the gash on Sean's head and closed it together with butterfly bandages.

"You need to get this stitched up, but otherwise you should be fine." The old EMT told Sean. Wendy was unharmed, but still a bit shaken up from the ordeal. "You should come to the hospital with us."

"No," Sean said. "I'll come by later, but I need to be here right now."

"Suit yourself," the older EMT said, "but you need to get that stitched up before it opens again." The EMTs closed up the ambulance and drove away.

Jason pulled into the parking lot on his bike as

the ambulance was pulling out. The club members, Sean, Wendy, and all of the police officers that were inside the clubhouse could hear the motorcycle engine as Jason pulled into the parking lot. They all filed out of the clubhouse one by one to meet him. Sean found himself praying that he would see Alex on the back of the motorcycle with Jason. They were all wishing for the same thing. They were all disappointed. Jason stopped in front of the clubhouse and sat on the bike facing everyone. No one knew what to say to him as he sat slumped on the back of his motorcycle. He shook his head to them.

"I couldn't get her."

Ron stepped out to the front of the group, "That's alright. *We* will. Together." He offered his hand to his son. Jason looked up into his father's face; Ron nodded to him. Jason took the offered hand and climbed off his bike.

Later, after the police had taken everyone's statements and left, the club had a meeting in their conference room. The men all sat in their usual seats around the table. Wendy was allowed to sit in on this meeting partly because she was a key witness and partly because Sean wouldn't let her out of his sight.

"They all had Reaper tattoos on their arms." Sean said and Wendy nodded her head in agreement.

"Everyone except Nate," she added.

"I didn't notice Nate's arm," Sean said.

"She's right," Jason said. "He didn't have a Reaper tattoo anywhere on him."

"What does that mean?" Wendy asked.

"It means," Bobby answered, "he's not a member yet. They used him to get to Alex. Wade knew Alex would never talk to anyone with a Reaper tattoo. He must have promised membership to Nate if he could find a way to get to us."

Ron nodded, "Wade is smart. Why do you think it's been so hard to get rid of the Reaper's Sons? This ends now." He turned to Wendy, "Is there anything else you remember that can help us? Any of you?"

"She said something to me when I tried to get her out of the van," Jason spoke up.

"Wait, what?" Kip asked. "You tried to pull her out of the van?" Jason relayed the story of him chasing after Alex to the rest of the club. "She was gonna jump?"

Jason nodded, "I'm pretty sure that if Nate hadn't pushed her she would've tried it."

"You're both insane."

"You said she told you something," Bobbie interrupted.

"She said 'Call Donnie.'"

"Donnie?" someone asked.

"Why Donnie?" Leo asked. Jason shook his head. He had been trying to figure that out since she told him.

"Donnie is good with computers," Wendy stated.

"So?" someone said.

"So...so maybe Alex knew that he would be able to find her."

"How?" Sean asked.

"I don't know. Just think about it, of all things to say to you she tells you to call Donnie. Why of all people would she choose Donnie? We all know Alex well enough to know that if she says something like that she obviously has a reason. I'm calling Donnie."

"You can do what you want, but I'm going to the basement to talk to that guy I knocked out." Jason said and he got up and left the room.

"Um, actually I'm the one who knocked him out," Sean called after him.

"Really Sean?" Wendy asked.

"He only distracted him, then I got up and knocked him out."

"Does it matter?"

"I'm just saying."

"Stop, please." Wendy told him. She left the room and called Donnie on her cell phone. He said he would be there as fast as he could and she told him to walk right in and come to the meeting room at the end of the hallway.

Downstairs Jason was sitting in a chair directly across from the man that Sean was claiming to have knocked unconscious. "Man" didn't seem to be the right word to describe him. He was much younger than the Reapers Jason knew and fought against. He couldn't have been more than 19 years old. His hands were tied with rope and his mouth was taped shut. Sean had been afraid that he would make noise and alert the police officers that he was there.

"I'm going to ask you a few questions. I ask, you answer. If I think you're lying at all I'm going to punch you in the face. Understand?" The hostage nodded. "Good. I know you're a Reaper, but who are you?" Jason reached down and ripped the tape off the guy's mouth.

"My name is Mike."

"Alright then Mike, Who's idea was it to come here?"

"I don't know." Mike's head whipped sideways as Jason backhanded him across the left side of his face. "His name is Nate or something like that."

"It was his idea?"

Mike nodded, "He wants to be a Reaper. Wade doesn't like him, but he thought it was a good opportunity to finally get to you guys. Nate didn't have any tattoos and none of you knew him. He was supposed to get close to your club somehow and find a weakness?"

"What did he find?"

"He came back a few weeks after he left sayin' that some girl was the key to bringin' you guys down."

"Alex."

Mike nodded again, "He said that your club protected her. That they would do anything for her and her sister. He said that if we kidnapped her that we would be able to negotiate anything we wanted from you and you would have no choice but to cooperate."

"What did they want from us?"

"I don't know," Jason raised his hand, "No wait! Really man, I don't know what they wanted. I mean I'm not sure. They said something about maybe getting you to negotiate to let them bring the drugs in through the town. Or something about you not interfering with their business anymore. That's all I know."

"Where did they take her?"

"They said they were gonna take her to some place where they didn't think you'd be able to find her. It was a cabin somewhere off the main roads, but I wasn't told where. I was just supposed to help grab her and then follow them to the cabin. You gotta believe me."

"I do." Jason said. He stood to leave.

"Wait." Jason turned back to him. "What are you gonna do with me?"

"How old are you?"

"Seventeen."

"Wade let you patch in at seventeen? Why?"

"I grew up in his town. I never really wanted to be a Reaper, but my father was a Reaper. He was Wade's best friend and the Vice President of the club. My dad got killed in some stupid bar fight like five years ago and ever since then Wade has taken care of me and my mom. I didn't have a choice. They made me run errands and do favors for them at first."

"You mean like that night we found you

selling drugs?"

"That was the first time I did anything with drugs, but yeah. Once they realized that I was actually pretty good at doing what they told me, they voted me in as a member." He paused, "You can't let me go back there. They'll kill me!"

"What makes you think that?"

"The other guys know that I never left the parking lot with them. They either think I'm dead or that you guys questioned me. If I turn up alive they'll know that you questioned me and they'll never trust that I didn't betray them. The last guy that betrayed them ended up dead in a way that I don't ever want to happen to me."

"Would you be willing to help us?"

"I never wanted to be a Reaper, it was just expected. My mom is single and works two jobs. I thought I would be able to make money to help us, but I've seen things. I don't want to go back there."

"What if I offered you a deal?"

"I'd take it. I don't even care what it is just help me."

"Help me find Alex and get her home safe and I promise you will never have to go back to their town. I promise that you and your mother can move into this town and never be judged for what you've done."

"You'll do that for me?"

"Help me and I swear it."

"Then I'll swear to help you no matter what."

Ten minutes later Donnie crawled out of his metallic blue Chevy Tahoe with spinning rims and a huge stereo system set up in the back, carrying a laptop satchel bag over his shoulder and walked into the Fu Lions clubhouse. He went to the meeting room in the back as Wendy had instructed him to over the phone. When he walked into the room he found the entire Fu Lions club sitting around their meeting table. He had only been in this room once a long time ago and absolutely nothing had been changed since then; it was exactly as he remembered it.

"Donnie, finally," Wendy said as he entered the room.

"I came as fast as I could," he said.

"We need you to help us answer a question," Ron said from the head of the table.

"Sure, what can I do?"

"You can tell us why, just as she is being dragged away at gunpoint, Alex would tell me to call you of all people." Jason said. He entered the room behind Donnie with Mike in tow. Mike's hands were untied and he also was bleeding from a head wound.

"What's he doing in here?" Dennis said.

"It's ok," Jason said. "He's going to help us. His name is Mike and he's only seventeen. Wade blackmailed him into becoming a Reaper, by using his Mom's money troubles against him. He's promised to help us in exchange for full protection for him and his mother against the Reapers."

The others remained silent. They were uneasy about trusting a Reaper. Wendy was the first to speak up.

"You're bleeding," she said. "Let me see what I can do to help. Are you thirsty?"

Mike nodded, "Could I have a glass of water?

Please."

"Of course." Wendy disappeared out the door and came back holding a glass of water and the first aid kit. "Drink up and let me take a look at you." Sean stood up and offered his chair to Mike. Mike sat down and drank his water as Wendy cleaned the cut on his head. "I think that you may need stitches too later today. These should do the trick for now." She closed the wound with two butterfly bandages, the same as Sean's, and put the first aid kit back. The men around the table seemed to soften towards Mike the longer they watched him. They saw what Jason had seen: that he was young for his age, young and scared.

"Alright Donnie, your turn," Bobbie said. "Why you?"

"A couple weeks ago Alex stopped by my house. It was a couple days after the cookout at her house. She brought me her cell phone. She told me that she was afraid that the Reaper's would come for her again."

"That's what she was doing?" Kip asked.

"You knew about this?" Jason asked.

Kip shook his head, "No, I mean I knew she went to Donnie's, I took her there. I didn't know what they were doing because she made me wait outside."

"She knew the whole time that this would happen," Jason said. "She told me several times. We tried to protect her, but I think she knew it wouldn't be enough."

"I don't think she thought the club couldn't protect her. There was something else in her face when she came to me that day. Like she knew she would give herself up to protect the club."

Wendy nodded, "When we were surrounded in this room, before Sean and Jason got to us, she surrendered herself and told them she would go with them. She was trying to prevent something happening to me."

"She did the same thing in the van," Jason added. "She knew that if she jumped out of that van that they'd just come back for her again. She gave herself up. She was trying to end this on her own." Jason turned around and punched a hole in the wall.

"I should have known what she was doing."

"It's not your fault Jason," Wendy said. "What did she want you to do for her Donnie?"

"She made me put a tracer in her cell phone. One that couldn't be seen or detected by a bug finder. It is designed to stay on if the phone is off or destroyed, it even works when it's wet." Donnie set his laptop bag on the table and pulled out of his laptop gear. "She made me set it up so that only I could trace her and only through this laptop." Donnie typed in, what looked like complete gibberish to everyone else in the room, until a map appeared on the computer screen with a bright yellow dot in the center. "There. She's in the middle of the woods off the main road 20 miles outside of town."

The men all crowded around Donnie's computer.

"Smart girl," Kip repeated from earlier. "Let's go get her."

Ron shook his head, "We can't. They're expecting us to come after her and fast. She's safer if we do nothing. Alex would want us to wait, to regroup, and to make a plan before we do anything."

"We can see where she is. We're looking right at her. We have to go get her."

"I agree with Ron," Leo said. "We have to be smart about this. Alex was smart and now we have to be."

"Can you message her through the computer like a text?" Ron asked Donnie.

Donnie nodded, "I can do anything with that phone through this laptop. I can turn her ringer on silent and send her a message."

"Do it. Text her: We know your location. Hang on. Text back if you are ok." Donnie did as he was asked. "How long do we have to wait?"

"I can't tell you. It all depends on when or if she'll be able to look at her phone and have time to respond. She might have been searched and had her phone taken away."

Wendy shook her head, "She knew what she was doing the whole time and had a plan set up in case this happened. There's no way she'll lose that phone. She'll text back."

"Wade is smart too," Jason said. "He's had his own plan the whole time too. He used Nate to find a weakness and now he's using Alex as leverage against us. He'll be calling soon to make some kind of demand." Jason explained what Mike had told him in the basement earlier, Mike filling in as many details as he could recall.

"Donnie, we need you to hang out with us here, I want to know the second Alex texts back or if that dot moves an inch," Ron ordered. "We all need to stay here and figure out our next move. Go and call your families, tell them you'll be coming home late tonight. Wendy you don't have to stay. Sean and Mike both need to go to the hospital."

"I'll take them," Wendy offered, "but then I'm coming back. I want to help. If it was me Alex wouldn't rest until I was back safe and I'm going to do the same for her."

"I want to help too," Mike added. "I'm sick of Wade thinking he controls me. I don't know Alex, but I do know that she's innocent and doesn't deserve anything they might do to her." He looked to Ron, "I think that I may have an idea and if you'll let me I'll tell you it when I come back."

Ron agreed that Wendy would take Sean and Mike to the hospital to get stitches and that they could return together to help make a plan to bring Alex home.

The only thing left for the men to do was make a plan and wait.

Chapter 13

Her hands were tied in front of her. The rope was tight around Alex's wrists, rubbing her skin raw and cutting off the circulation in her hands. It was nighttime now; darkness flooded into the locked room. She retied the loose strings on her sneakers, grateful that she had been smart enough to put them on that morning and wishing that she had taken the time to put on a pair of socks too. She had woken up to a day that felt like it was from a dream, but the dream had quickly faded into a nightmare.

She closed her eyes, but sleep was impossible. Instead she tried to recall as many details as she could about where she was. The ride here wasn't long, maybe 20 minutes, which meant she couldn't be that far outside of town. When the van had finally stopped, she was pulled out so fast she could barely take in her surroundings. She was able to catch glimpses of a log cabin, situated off the main roads and on the outskirts of woods.

There were at least 10 men on guard at the

cabin including the five that had brought her here. Six men were sent to bring her here: three on motorcycles, two in the van and one that didn't make it back. After Nate saved her from falling off the van door, he gagged her and tied her hands together tightly with rope. He wasn't going to let her surprise him again. He also kept the gun trained on her for the rest of the ride, never moving his eyes or attention from her. When they arrived at least four more men, that she could see, had been waiting at the cabin. Each one was heavily armed, carrying a machine gun in his hands, a 9mm holstered under his jacket, and she was willing to bet each one of them had a knife hidden somewhere on their person as well. Some of the men looked familiar to her, which was no surprise. Before they managed to lock her in this room she heard one of them mention more would be coming later that day. A small army guarding a log cabin and a single, twenty-two year old girl; it seemed ridiculous, but in reality it wasn't. The men knew the Fu Lions would be coming for her and they were smart to prepare. Nothing would be able to stop

Jason or any of the other members once they had a plan. Alex knew that, since they hadn't already come for her, they were waiting and making a plan. The thought calmed her, she knew that whatever they were planning the Reapers wouldn't be ready for it; they had unleashed something that they didn't have the strength to stop.

The Reapers had already made one crucial mistake when they brought her here; no one had thought to search her pockets when they grabbed her. She always carried her father's pocket knife wherever she went. The knife had been in her shorts pocket when the men picked her up, right next to her cell phone which she knew Donnie was tracing now or would be soon. The second the men left her in this locked room she jumped into action, knowing that soon enough they would come back and search her. She managed to hide both the knife and the cell phone under one of the loose floorboards in the corner of the room before Nate came back in.

She was sitting down in the opposite corner of the room across from the door, hoping that she would be able to keep his attention away from the cracked floor board where she hid the phone and the knife. He grabbed her wrists and pulled her up off the floor until she was standing in front of him. Nate smirked as he began to run his hands over her clothes checking all of her pockets and even inside her shirt. Nate continued to smirk even after he was finished. He stood facing her, his hands holding her tied wrists that were starting to bleed from the tight ropes.

"Did you shut the car door on your finger?" Alex asked sarcastically, looking at Nate's middle finger which was wrapped in a bandage.

Nate's smirk faded as he said, "You know you could have prevented all of this,"

"Oh? And how's that? If I agreed to go on another date with you, then you never would have betrayed me to the Reapers?"

"Wade sent me in to find your club's weakness. I could have told him it was anything, but the truth was that you and your sister are a weakness for the whole town. I didn't understand it at first, but the closer I got to you I realized that you had this way of tricking people into falling in love with you. I would've lied to protect you, but you barely gave me a second look. You only went out with me out of pity. Eventually you would have broken things off with me and would've gone running into your little Jason's arms."

"Jason never trusted you. I should have listened to him--he was right--but I did like you otherwise I never would have gone out with you. When Jason said he thought you might be the rat, I wanted to give you the benefit of the doubt. I gave you a chance and you blew it, you gave me up to the Reapers and now they're going to kill me. But you know what, I've decided I'm ok with that, they can kill me. Now I only need to live long enough to see Jason kill you.

"I could have protected you," he said. "You never gave me a chance."

She didn't respond, instead she stared him down, never breaking eye contact. He was much bigger than her and she knew she had no chance of overpowering him. Even if she did manage to bring him down, there were still nine more outside the door. No, she would wait; her time for revenge would come. Donnie would be tracing her cell phone any minute now and the club would know her location. They would come for her, Jason would come for her. She only hoped they wouldn't be too late.

Alex heard a commotion going on in the other room; at first she thought that the club had come for her, but as she listened to the voices she knew it wasn't them. From what she heard of the conversation the rest of the Reaper's club had arrived with reinforcements. There were so many voices in the cabin now, but only one stood out to Alex the most. Wade was definitely inside the cabin. She hadn't checked her cell phone yet for any messages from the club, but there was no way she would risk it now. There were too many footsteps moving around making it impossible for her to tell whether they were heading towards her room or not. She'd have to wait and see what the morning would bring.

An hour later, Wade came to see her. She was

sitting across from the doorway again, so that when he entered she was the first thing he saw. She stood as he came in. He shut the door behind him and leaned his back on it, not walking any further into the room. He stared at her for several minutes contemplating what to say.

He finally spoke saying, "So, we finally meet."

"You're Wade," she stated.

He nodded, "And you're Alex Murphy, the famous girl who has a whole town of people wrapped around her little finger. I hear they call you Al."

"My friends call me Al."

"What should I call you then?"

"Not a friend."

"Humph," he grunted with a sinister smirk.

"You planted Nate in the same school as me, paid his tuition to go there so that he could get close to me and find a weakness in the club. He told you that I was the club's weakness and you sent him to fetch me and bring me here."

"You're a smart girl."

"What did you think you would gain by bringing me here? If you thought for one second that the Lions would come here and offer to exchange our town for me, you were seriously mistaken. They will come here, but not to negotiate. They'll come here and they'll kill every one of you."

Wade shot across the room and slammed Alex against the wall, his hand wrapped around her throat. "It is *you* who's mistaken," he whispered, his face so close to hers that his lips were touching her ear as he spoke. "The Lions *will* come here and they *will* negotiate. Then I'm going to bring you out front and I'm going to shoot you in front of them. Then I'm going to kill them all. Did you think I wouldn't be prepared for them? All twenty-five members of the Reaper's Sons are outside this door. I also hired several men who shoot first and don't ask questions."

"Mercenaries."

Wade nodded, "Mercenaries," he continued to hold her pinned against the wall. "Your men are going to walk into an ambush that they will not win." He released her and stepped away. He stood in front of her and stared, "You look just like your mother," he said turning to leave the room.

"My mother? You knew my mother?"

"I'm not surprised they didn't tell you."

"What do you know about my mother?"

"Your mother wasn't from your little town like everyone's told you. She was from mine."

"What?"

"She grew up in my town. We were high school sweethearts, supposed to get married when we graduated. But your mother went and ruined everything. She broke down on the side of the road one day in the old junk box of a car she wouldn't let me replace. She was stuck on the road on the outskirts of your town without a cell phone. Some guy in a tow truck drove by and saw her. Offered to take her into town to the local auto shop and fix her car."

"My father."

"Your father. Kevin Murphy took her to Murphy Automotive and fixed her car. She came home and broke up with me a week later. They started dating in secret and fell in 'love.'" He used his fingers as air quotes as he spat out the word love. "He married her and took her away from my town. She could no longer be trusted. She knew too many secrets about the Reapers, I should know because I was the one who told her."

"You killed her," Alex could barely say the words.

"It was my mess and I had to clean it up. I took my best friend and we went to your house that night. We waited until you and your sister were in bed. Your father was telling you some bedtime story about the founding of your club. We walked right through the front door and I shot her." Tears started to fall down Alex's cheeks as she pulled the memory from the recesses of her mind. "Your father swore he'd find and kill us and he never gave up. He looked for us for years. One night he showed up in the same bar as us. He immediately recognized my best friend, who had come with me that night and had pinned your father down to the floor as I shot your mother. A fight broke out and your father and my friend killed each other leaving you and your sister orphaned and my best friend's son fatherless. I've helped raise that boy, made him a sort of pet for the guys in the club. An errand boy, now he's a full member. You're Uncle was even easier to take out. I slipped an untraceable poison in his drink at a bar one night. The poison made it look like he had a heart attack. Everyone believed the story given the fact that he had recently been put under a lot of stress, taking over the club and raising his brother's children."

Alex couldn't respond, couldn't stop the tears from falling. She wiped her face with her still tied-up hands, "Why didn't they tell me?"

Wade shrugged, "Like I said, I'm not surprised they didn't." He opened the door and started to step outside when Alex finally found her voice again.

"They were protecting me. They knew that I'd kill you."

"Humph," he grunted for the second time since he came in the room, "Guess it's too late for that now." He made to leave one last time.

"No. It's not. They're going to come here for

me and I'm going to get out of this room and when that happens I *will* kill you. I swear it."

Wade slammed the door shut behind him.

The clubhouse phone rang at 6:00; eight hours after the Reaper's took Alex. Wendy had taken Sean and Mike to the hospital so they could both get stitches on their heads, afterwards she drove them both back to the clubhouse. The three of them were sitting at a table in the bar with Jason who hadn't spoken much in the last couple of hours. The rest of the men were also sitting at tables and at the bar, they had already formed a plan in the meeting room earlier and now they were waiting. They were waiting to see if Alex or Wade would make contact. Mostly they didn't know what else to do with themselves. Sara, Audrey, and Carla with her girls and Jesse came over to the clubhouse as soon as they'd heard what happened. Donnie had stayed like he was asked, he sat at the bar counter in front of his laptop, staring at the yellow dot on the screen. The bar was full of solemn faces and silence as they all waited. They all jumped up when the phone rang. Jason was the fastest.

"Hello," he answered with force in his voice. "Wade," he said after a pause. He held the phone out to Ron, "He wants to speak to you." Ron took the phone without hesitation.

"Wade, I believe you have something that belongs to me," Ron answered. He set the phone down on the counter and put it on speaker so that everyone else could hear the conversation. He motioned for everyone to be silent as Wade began to speak.

"I'm willing to give her back," Wade said from the other end of the line, "for a price of course."

"Of course," Ron responded. "And what is it that you want?"

"I think you know what it is that I want."

"Yes, you're right. How do you propose that we make this exchange?"

"Tomorrow morning. 11:00. I will text you an address. Come unarmed and you will get what you want."

"How do I know she is alright? I want to talk to her."

"As you wish."

A moment later they heard Alex's voice, "Uncle Ronnie?"

"Alex, are you alright?"

"I'm fine. Is Wendy ok?"

"I'm alright," Wendy spoke up.

"Am I on speaker phone?" Alex asked.

"Yes," Jason responded. "We are all here Alex. Sean, Wendy, Donnie, the club, Jesse, we're all at the bar waiting to hear from you."

He was sending her a message and she understood clearly. He was telling her that he had found Donnie and that they were waiting for her to text them through his computer. "My sister is there?"

"I'm here, Alex," Jesse said.

"Jesse remember my promise?"

Jesse was crying as she answered, "Yes."

"I want you to know that I intend to keep it. I love you Jesse. I love all of you. Promise me you won't do anything foolish. I know that I'm going to be ok." The phone was ripped away from her ear as she finished her last sentence.

"Satisfied?" Wade asked.

"Far from it," Ron responded.

"Be at the address at 11:00 sharp or she's dead."

The line went dead.

Eleven o'clock tomorrow morning. That was the deadline for Alex's life. She waited until she knew Wade would not be coming back again before she ran to the corner where her cell phone was stashed. She struggled to reopen the floor board with her hands still tied, as quietly as she could. She slipped her hands underneath the board and grabbed hold of her cell phone. When she pushed the side button on the phone the screen lit up with an alert telling her there was a text message waiting.

We know your location. Hang on. Text back if you are ok—FL

The message had been sent only two hours after she had arrived at the cabin. She hated that she hadn't had a chance to respond yet. She knew Ron would have Donnie monitoring the computer all night. She quickly wrote back:

Am ok. What's the plan? --A

She held the phone in her lap while she waited for a response. Just as she thought the screen lit up shortly after her message was sent. The new message said:

We will ambush them tomorrow at the exchange. Any details will help. --J

The conversation continued on:

Cabin is surrounded by woods--good for cover. 25 Reaper's on guard plus several hired mercenaries. Wade is going to pretend to make a deal and then kill me in front of you. I'm in back room with two windows. Hands tied. Can use pocket knife to cut ropes. —A

Cut the ropes at 11:00, but get down. Don't leave the back room, we will be firing from both sides. Just get down and I will come in and get you. Try to rest. I will text you in the morning. Be ready when I say. --J

Are you alone Jason? --A

Yes. Everyone has gone home. Getting ready for tomorrow. Donnie left the computer with me --J

Promise me something? --A

Anything. —J

If the worst happens promise me you will take care of Jesse.—A

I promise that it won't come to that. —J

Jason, I've had a good life. I want you to know that I regret nothing that I've done except never saying goodbye to my parents. I don't want that to happen to us. You have always been my best friend. Thank you for everything that you and your family have done for me and Jesse. Take care of her. --A

I will, I promise. You have been the most important person in my life. I will do anything to bring you home tomorrow. I will not say goodbye, there is no need. Stop being silly. I will see you at 11:00. Be ready. --J

Thank you Jason. See you at 11:00. --A

Jason had told her to rest and so she tried. She put the phone back under the floor and then curled up on the floor beside it. When Jason texted her in the morning she would do everything she could to be ready like he asked. She had to find a way to cut the rope from around her wrists with her knife, but that would have to wait until morning. She fully intended to listen to what Jason had told her to do. *Cut the ropes and get down,* is what he wanted her to do. She hoped it would be as simple as that, but feared it wouldn't. If Wade even got a hint that things weren't going to go his way the first thing he would do would be to come into the room and kill her. He might not get the satisfaction of doing it in front of the Lions, but it would make him the winner. It didn't matter who or how many died in the fight tomorrow, the only way Wade could win was with her death. She had to stay alive to save her club, to save her town, to be with her sister again. She would have to fight because she refused to die.

Chapter 14

Jason woke up early having barely slept the night before. Today was the day that would end a war that had been going on long before he and Alex were even born. Today was going to be the most important day in his life. The rest of his life would be determined by what happened to him today.

He dressed in black pants and a tight black t-shirt with the Lion's logo on the back. This was the outfit they had all agreed upon when making their plan the night before. They wanted to look like a single unit when they attacked the cabin. He looked at the clock in the kitchen which read 7:00 am. Two hours until the rest of the guys got to the clubhouse, four hours until their meet at the cabin. He dissembled two of his guns and cleaned them slowly, making sure to wipe down every inch of the gun. He couldn't afford to have any problems with his gun today

The Fu Lions club members began to arrive at 9:00. They were dressed alike as planned. By 9:15

they were all there, including Mike, Donnie, Wendy, and all of the women attached to the club. The men brought every weapon that they had to the clubhouse and placed it on the table in the meeting room. It took them an hour to get ready. Donnie sat in a chair in the center of the table and reopened the GPS on Alex's cell phone through his laptop. He pulled up the satellite image of the cabin.

"Guys, we have a problem," he said.

"What do you mean?" Ron asked.

"Come see for yourself."

Ron walked around the table until he can see the computer screen. The cabin was surrounded on all sides by red heat signatures. There were at least twenty men surrounding the outside of the cabin and a big red area on the inside indicating a large number of people inside in the front of the cabin. In the back left corner of the cabin there was only one small red person all by themselves. Alex.

"What's wrong?" Jason asked his father.

"There are a lot of men at that cabin."

"I told you that last night after I heard from

Alex."

"Yes, but they are positioned on all sides. There are five guarding the back windows into the room where Alex is, we'll never be able to break her out that way like we planned." Jason joined his father and Bobbie on the other side of the computer.

"This doesn't change anything," Jason said. "We still go along with the plan, only we don't try and pull Alex out through the windows. There's a side door into the cabin. Instead my group will come in from that side and go through the door. I told Alex to get down as soon as she heard us coming, so she should be safe. The door isn't heavily guarded because they're expecting us to try to get to her out the other way. They just made our job easier."

"Jason, we don't know exactly how many are inside," Dennis said.

"Nor will we when the time comes, but I'm willing to bet that when this starts Wade will have most of the men guarding him and Alex, they won't be looking for us on the sides, only in the back and the front."

"Are you willing to bet all of our lives on it?"

Jason nodded, "Yes."

"What about her life?"

Jason thought for a moment, "I know Alex better than any of you. I know that if it were me in there then she would place the same bet."

The answer was enough. The men all strapped their guns on their bodies, put on their Fu Lions leather jackets and went out into the bar to say goodbye to the women.

"Be careful," Wendy said to Sean.

"I will be. I promise."

Wendy wiped her eye before a tear could fall, "I feel like I just got you back. You go in there and you get Alex and then you come back to me. Do you hear me? No matter what, you come back to me."

"I love you, Wendy," Sean kissed her.

"I love you too."

Sean kissed her one last time and then walked out the front door.

Ron wrapped Sara into his arms. "Bring her home," she whispered into his leather jacket. Jesse was standing beside her, Ron pulled her into their embrace.

"I will," he said back. Jason approached from behind and they welcomed him into a family hug.

"I have to do this, Mom. She'd do the same for any of us."

Sara nodded, "I know. Be careful." She held a silent Jesse by the shoulders as she watched her husband and son follow the others out the front door.

As Jason followed the others out, he turned for a moment and made eye contact with the young Reaper, Mike. Mike was standing near the doorway watching as everyone said their goodbyes and left. Mike nodded to Jason who nodded back. They had a mutual understanding with each other; both were fighting for the woman they loved; Mike was fighting to protect his mother and Jason was fighting to bring Alex home. Jason joined the others out front where the motorcycles were all parked in a line. Together they mounted the bikes and started the engines.

The sight could be seen by anyone who was on the main street of the town. All of the Fu Lions were lined up on their bikes in the clubhouse parking lot. The engines all started at once roaring in unison like a heard of lions after their prey. That is what they were: Lions. The women joined them out front as they pulled away. People from town heard the engines and looked out their front windows to watch as they pulled away. Some joined them in the street waving goodbye as they watched the bikes pull out of the parking lot and disappear down the road. Most in town knew the reason they were leaving and all were praying for their safe return.

The sunlight from the windows woke Alex from her sleep, before she even opened her eyes. For a moment she believed that she was back in Jason's apartment on top of the bar and that he was lying next to her, but as she rolled over the hard floor reminded her of where she really was. The floor had made her stiff and kept her awake through most of the night. She managed to drift off for a couple of hours, but it wasn't enough. She was exhausted and she desperately needed her strength for what was to come.

She wanted to text Jason before the exchange and fight began, but she wasn't willing to risk getting caught with her phone. Any hint of what was to come and Wade would kill her and take his men and leave. No, this had to end today. She sat up and leaned her back against the wall. She stretched her arms above her head and yawned shaking the stiffness from her limbs. She put her legs out straight in front of her and reached for her toes. She stood up and stretched down touching her toes again. She stretched until her entire body felt loose and ready and then she sat back down in her place to wait.

It was still early; she guessed around eight o'clock in the morning. She could hear the men moving around in the cabin, the banging of guns on a table, and the sharpening of a blade. The noise was loud enough that it would cover the sound of her pulling up the floor board. She could stand it no longer and decided she would risk it. She crawled over to the far corner and pulled up the floor board.

She retrieved both her phone and her pocket knife and then slid the board back into place. She would have to find a way to hide both items on her because she wanted to be ready when the fight began; she didn't want to have to worry about pulling them out of the floor again. She took the knife and slid it inside her sneaker. It wasn't comfortable, but it would have to do for now. She pushed the side button on the phone to light up the screen. The clock told her that it was 8:30. Only two and a half hours to wait.

She didn't know what the plan was, only that she was supposed to get down during the shooting. To her that meant that the club was planning to come from all sides. She stood up and looked out of the room's window. There were five men standing outside at different intervals all facing the woods. If Jason was going to try to come from that side he'd never make it without getting someone hurt. She knew Donnie could pull up a satellite image of the cabin, so the club must have seen that it would be impossible to try that way. They must have figured out a better way to come and get her. The only other way out of this room was the door, which would be suicide if she tried it herself now, but during the fight with her men inside, it might be possible. She needed to come up with her own back-up plan in case things went wrong. She had a few ideas, but would have to wait until the timing was right to choose which one was best. For now she just had to wait.

Ron and Jason led the men down the road. It was exactly a twenty minute ride to the cabin. They had left the clubhouse at 9:00, which meant they would arrive at the cabin too early, but that wasn't the plan. Five minutes before they reached the cabin they reached a small dirt road, nearly concealed by trees. They took it and followed it deep into the woods. The road lead them almost all the way to the cabin, but allowed them to remain unseen. They stopped and turned their engines off so as not to alert the men at the cabin. Ron would meet with Wade in front of the cabin with Leo, Kip and Dennis. Jason, Sean, Bobbie, Russell, and all the other men were staying here in the woods and surrounding the cabin. Ron was the distraction and Jason would lead the assault. It was dangerous for both of them, but neither gave giving up a second thought.

The men began positioning themselves as planned, around the cabin. Jason was sitting behind a tree that was directly in front of the side door where he would be breaking into the cabin. They had to wait another thirty minutes before Ron could leave for the meet. Jason pulled his cell phone out of his pocket. There were no incoming texts. He found Alex's number on the phone and sent her a new text message:

We are here. Ron and Wade meet at exactly 11:00. When you hear gunshots, get down. --J

There are too many men outside the window, you can't come that way. --A

We know. We are coming in from a side door. Remember Alex, just get down and I'll come and get you. --J

See you at 11:00. --A

Jason didn't like the last text she sent. She never promised him or gave her word that she would stay out of the fight and that scared him. He wanted to text her again to make her promise, but he knew the longer she stayed on the phone the bigger the risk. He could only hope that she didn't do anything foolish.

Ron approached him a few minutes later. It was time for Kip, Leo and him to leave. Jason stood and shook his father's hand. Ron pulled him into one more hug.

"Be careful," Ron told his son. "You're mother will kill me if anything happens to you."

"You be careful too, Dad. She'll be just as mad at me if something happens to you."

Kip and Leo also shook hands with Jason and then followed Ron over to where they had left the motorcycles. They had to go in unarmed. Wade would have them searched the minute they stepped foot on the property. Jason didn't like the fact that they would be defenseless if things went wrong, but there was no choice. Jason would just have to do his job right so that they all could go home.

Chapter 15

At exactly 11:00 Wade heard three motorcycle engines pull down the driveway to the cabin. He stepped outside the front door to greet his rivals. Six men went out front with him. Wade waited until Ron and his men climbed off their bikes and took off their helmets before he spoke.

"Right on time," he said looking at his watch.

"I've come to collect what belongs to me," Ron replied. He raised his arms in the air to show that he carried no weapon. Leo and Kip followed his lead exactly as Wade's men kept their guns trained on the three of them. Wade motioned for his men to check the Lions for weapons. Leo and Kip allowed the men to search them without making a fuss.

"Humph," Wade said as the men were being searched. "Belongs to you? What gives you a right to that girl?"

"Her family asked me to take care of her in the event of their deaths, since you killed her family off I have gained the right to watch over her."

"Well I tell you what: if you give me your little town and promise to not interfere with our business anymore, I'll gladly give her back to you."

"Fine, take the town. Now I want to see her."

"Tsk, Tsk, Tsk, did you really think it would be that simple? You came here unarmed with only two other men and here I am with an entire army. I have to say I'm a little disappointed in you really. What makes you think that I won't just kill you all and take the town for myself?"

It was a test. Wade was trying to learn if the Lions had other plans; Ron knew this and simply answered, "Nothing is stopping you."

Wade stared at him. He seemed satisfied with Ron's response, "Very well. Bring me the girl," he ordered his men.

Then he heard a gunshot.

What Wade didn't know was that as he was talking to Ron, Jason and his men had approached the cabin quietly holding off on using their guns for as long as they possibly could. First they took out the three men guarding the side door. Next they were supposed to go after the five men standing guard outside the windows to the room Alex was in, but like Alex predicted, that point of entry was impossible to attack without alerting the others. That was where the first gunshot came from. Russell and Bobbie led four others to that side of the cabin, but during the commotion one of the Lions was forced to shoot his gun.

Jason heard the shot and knew that he had to hurry now. Sean followed him to the cabin's side door. There were shots being fired everywhere now. Five men came running out of the side door where Jason and Sean were waiting for them. The men were easily picked off and Jason was slowly getting closer and closer to being able to enter the cabin.

Inside the cabin, Alex heard the gunshot. Seconds before the attack began Jason texted her one last time. The message was only one word: *Now*. She immediately pulled the knife out of her shoe and began working on the ropes around her wrists. She held the knife between her sneakered feet and ran the rope up and down the blade. It was tiresome and took a long time to do, but finally she managed to get free from the ropes. The instant the ropes broke off her hands the first shot had been fired. She threw the ropes to the side and got down beside the door. The door opened out away from the room and would provide no cover for her if someone entered, but she hoped that crouching beside it would give her an edge that whoever came in wouldn't expect.

She could hear shots being fired from every direction now. One of the bullets came through the side window and into her room. The glass shattered and burst into the room flying in every direction. Alex was far enough away from the windows so the glass couldn't reach her. She heard the men inside frantically running around trying to save themselves. She wasn't surprised later when she learned that a few of the men deserted their so-called brothers and disappeared into the woods.

Alex was beginning to believe that Wade wouldn't come for her like she feared. It had been several minutes of gunfire and still she sat alone in this room. She remained where she was as the guns continued to fire and bullets ricocheted into the room through the windows. Then slowly the door into the room began to open.

After Wade heard the first gun go off, he immediately pulled out his gun and aimed it at Ron. He fired his weapon, but when he looked up Ron still remained standing. Kip and Leo managed to overpower two of Wade's men and each got their hands on a weapon. Wade realized that even though he still had the numbers, he would be in great danger if he remained out front. Ron overpowered another one of Wade's men, leaving only three plus Nate and Wade. Wade stood by the front door and watched as the men fought. All was lost he thought to himself, but then he remembered that he still had the upper hand. He still had Alex.

He motioned for Nate to follow him back inside the cabin. The men inside were shooting out the windows aiming at targets hidden in the woods.

Wade had to duck down a few times to avoid being hit by the bullets flying in through the windows. Nate followed close at his heels until they reached the back room where they had Alex stashed.

"Wait here," Wade told Nate. "If I don't come out of this room, kill whoever does." Nate nodded in understanding.

Slowly Wade began to open the door.

Chapter 16

Alex remained crouched in her position, her weight centered on the balls of her feet, as she watched Wade take a small step into the room. She could see the confusion on his face as he noticed the ropes that were previously tied around her wrists, lying in the middle of the floor. She could also see that he was carrying a gun. He hadn't noticed her yet; she held as still as she could forcing herself to breath as quietly as possible. When Wade took another step into the room she shot out with her arm and shoved her knife as far into his right leg as she could. He howled in pain and stepped sideways, further into the room, slamming the door shut. Alex stood and lashed out at the hand holding his gun. The gun flew across the floor and landed in the center of the room. Wade bent over and pressed his hands around the knife jutting from his leg. Alex stood over Wade as he struggled to remove the knife.

"I made you a promise that I intend to keep," she told him.

Wade looked up at her and snarled like a wild animal when it's wounded. He pulled the knife out of his leg slowly, grunting in pain as it came free. The knife made a sloshing noise as it tore loose from his leg and soaked his jeans with blood. He stood up straight so that they were eye to eye clutching the small pocket knife in his large hand. He lunged after her in an attempt to pin her against the wall, but she saw it coming. She ducked beneath him and he slammed into the wall behind her, but not before he managed to slice the side of her arm with the knife. He turned to face her again; they were both bleeding now. His jeans red from the thigh down to his knee and blood had started to drip down Alex's arm staining Jason's white shirt. She kicked out with her foot and managed to free the knife from his hand. They were both completely unarmed now. The surprise from her kick was registered all over Wade's face. He was getting frustrated and Alex knew it. He thought this would be an easy kill, how hard could it be to shoot a girl in the head and kill her? The more frustrated he got the less he would be able to focus on the fight.

Alex was standing poised to fight: knees slightly bent, arms up, palms open, the way she had once been taught by her Uncle Jim. After seeing the aggravation written all over Wade's face, she stood up straight and dropped one of her arms. The other arm she left up, stretching out toward him. She smirked as she turned her wrist over and made a "Come here" motion with her index finger. It was enough. Wade lunged at her again, only this time he didn't miss. The motion caused them both to fall to the floor together. Wade jumped up first and kicked Alex in the stomach as she tried to stand. The kick forced her to roll to her side. Wade came at her kicking her again and again until she had rolled across the entire floor and was lying in the middle of the room. Her stomach was killing her and she was sure that he cracked some of her ribs. She couldn't stand up. Wade walked over to where the knife had fallen on the floor and picked it up. He crossed the room so that he was standing above Alex looking down at her. He studied the knife, turning it over in his hands.

"Ironic isn't it?" He asked her. "The blade that once protected your father is the blade that is now going to kill you."

Wade kneeled down, his legs straddling her to hold her in place as he lifted the knife above his head with both hands. Alex felt the cool edges of metal, but it wasn't the knife, it was the gun. She wrapped her hand around the gun as Wade's hands began to quickly descend with the knife.

The knife was only inches away from her chest when she managed to pull the trigger. She fired the gun three times into his stomach. Wade moved his arms out to the sides and glanced at his stomach, a look of bewilderment covered his face as he looked from his stomach to Alex and then back again. She wriggled out from under him and began to inch away. Wade looked down and clutched his stomach with both hands. He was wearing a black shirt, so it was impossible to see how much blood there was until he pulled a drenched hand away. He stared into his bloodied hand and then looked back at Alex.

"Ironic isn't it?" She sat up from the floor and

shrugged her shoulders.

Wade fell backwards onto the floor and closed his eyes.

Alex took a second to catch her breath. She continued to hold the gun out in front of her, too shocked to move, afraid that Wade would jump up and attack her again. She didn't have the strength to stand yet but she built up the courage to crawl over to where he was laying. She was certain he was dead and didn't bother to check his neck for a pulse. She suddenly had a feeling of complete relief fall over her. It was finally done. Her family had been avenged and her father's oath had been fulfilled. All those years, almost her entire life, spent searching for her mother's killer had come to an end in an old abandoned cabin in the middle of nowhere. Wade was still clutching her father's knife tightly in his left hand, she pried his fingers open and reclaimed her knife. The blade was still covered with Wade's blood from when she stabbed him in the leg with it. She used the bottom edge of her shirt to wipe the blade clean. Jason's white shirt was stained red from where she cleaned the blade and from where Wade had sliced her arm with the knife. She lifted the shirt sleeve to inspect her arm. The blade had grazed her, but not badly enough to need stitches. Her arm continued to bleed as she rolled the sleeve back over it and applied pressure to the cut. The cut didn't hurt very much, but her stomach was turning with pain.

She could hear the fighting in the next room; could hear the voices of her friends. They must have broken through and gotten inside, she thought. Technically she was supposed to stay in this back room and wait until Jason came for her, but she couldn't bear staying in the room with Wade's body staring her in the face any longer. She checked the gun to see how many bullets she had left--only five left in the clip, she would have to make them count-- and then reloaded the clip back into the gun. She took another deep breath that hurt from the cracked ribs, and opened the door into the cabin.

Chaos. That was the first word that came to her mind as she studied the scene before her. She could only tell the men apart by the insignia on their jackets. The cabin was huge; the main area filled with fighting men. The entire cabin was one giant room with only a bathroom and the room she was locked in, off on the sides. There were windows on every wall and two doors: the front door and one on the side where The Lions seemed to be coming from. She spotted Sean, Dennis, Bobbie, and a few others amidst the chaos. They were each fighting someone one on one. Guns were being fired from every direction, bullets flying everywhere. She desperately looked for Jason, but she couldn't see him.

"Jason!" she yelled out hoping to attract his attention from somewhere in the room.

"Alex?" She heard his voice yell back. She called his name again and this time when he responded she saw where he was. He was on the opposite side of the room from her. He caught sight of her at the same time and began to move towards her.

Alex took a step forward out of the doorway of the room she had been locked in and felt a blow on her right side. Her arm immediately began to ache and she barely managed to hold on to the gun. She looked to the right and saw Nate standing beside her. Wade must have posted him there in case something happened and he didn't come out of the room, she thought. She stepped back from him and pointed her gun to his chest. He raised his own gun and aimed it at her head. They were in a standoff, neither one willing to take the risk of shooting the other. She looked to her left and could see Jason still trying to get over to her side of the cabin. She looked back at Nate who grinned. She was stuck, unable to do anything until someone could come and help her. She felt a bullet whiz by her and instinctively ducked down. Nate was forced to do the same as another bullet grazed the side of his arm. Alex used the opportunity to move as far away from him as she could. She dodged more bullets and pushed past fighting men, hoping to meet Jason somewhere in the middle of the room.

Nate moved to follow her, but was stopped by someone behind him. Alex saw Sean pull on Nate's shirt collar forcing him backwards. Sean nodded for Alex to keep moving as Nate regained his balance and lunged toward Sean. Alex saw Nate punch Sean in the face, throwing him off balance and forcing him to drop his gun. Alex aimed her gun and shot Nate in the arm in an attempt to give Sean more time. Nate went down as the bullet passed through his left arm. Sean quickly stood up and took hold of his gun. Alex was about to approach and help him again, when she felt a hand on her arm. She turned around and pointed her gun at the person touching her only to see that it was Jason. Relief flooded her. Jason pulled her body towards him and forced her into a kiss, blocking out the world around them.

"You alright?" He yelled over the gunfire. A worried expression covered his face as he noticed the amount of blood on her shirt.

"I'm fine," she said.

"You were supposed to stay put."

"I couldn't, Wade..." she stopped as Jason shot a Reaper over her shoulder. "Wade came for me."

"Where is he?"

"He didn't make it."

Jason raised his eyebrows at Alex and she shrugged back. "Do you have an extra clip?" she asked him. "I only have four rounds left." Jason reached into his jacket pocket and pulled out an extra magazine for Alex to use. She took it from him and easily slipped it into her gun as he stood in front of her to cover her.

"This is going to be rough, you ready?" He asked. Alex nodded. "Alex I have to tell you something now, just in case. I should have said it last night when I texted you, but I wanted to say it to you in person. I..."

"Hold that thought," Alex said as she aimed her gun at someone approaching him from behind. She shot and the man went down.

"Thanks, I..." Jason was forced to stop again as another man started coming at them from the side. Jason rolled his eyes and fired his gun. There were too many of them. Alex was standing on his right, shooting her gun towards another Reaper. Jason wasn't paying much attention when someone snuck up in between the two of them. The man grabbed Jason from behind, surprising him. The man was much bigger than he was, but Jason was able to overpower him. When he was sure the man was down he turned towards Alex again. She wasn't there. He frantically looked around for her, but couldn't find her.

When the man came between them, they had been too easily separated. Jason and the man fought towards the left side of the room and Alex was pushed towards the right. She kept firing her gun at the Reapers as they moved towards her. She was doing well, but knew that she would run out of bullets fast if this continued. She knew that Jason would have plenty more bullets and maybe even an extra gun. She needed to get back to him; together they were much stronger. She turned back to where they had been standing, but Jason was lost in the chaos.

"Looking for someone?" Alex turned to face Nate who was standing close behind her, sneering.

"Not you," she responded.

She lashed out with her leg and managed to

kick him in the stomach. The kick was not very strong, but gave her an advantage as Nate had to fight to keep his balance. He bounced back quickly and knocked the gun out of her hands. He was too strong for her, she knew she'd never be able to overpower him on her own. She tried to move towards her gun on the floor, but Nate was faster. He reached for her arm and flung her in the opposite direction. Alex reached into her pocket for her knife, but Nate anticipated her again and slapped her in the face. Her cheek burned red both from the slap and from embarrassment. She had beaten him before and knew she could again.

She pushed him forward and kneed him in his stomach. As Nate doubled over in pain he punched Alex aiming for her face, but landing in her stomach. He managed to hit her in just the right spot. She cried out in pain and crumpled to the floor. If her ribs were cracked earlier then they were certainly broken now. She lay on her side on the floor. Nate caught his breath and began to move in her direction. She crawled on the floor looking for the gun she had dropped earlier. She found it and rolled onto her back aiming the gun at Nate. She slowly squeezed the trigger, but nothing happened. Nate laughed at her and she desperately looked for the safety switch. The safety lock was in the off position. She cocked the gun and checked the clip; it was empty. She was out of bullets. Nate laughed at her again and then lunged after her. He grabbed her by both arms and pulled her up so she was standing in front of him. Her ribs were on fire and she was completely defenseless.

Nate was planning on shooting her and would have if Jason hadn't resurfaced at that moment. He yelled Alex's name and pointed his gun at Nate. Nate stepped behind Alex and used her as a shield holding his gun against her temple. Jason couldn't get a clear shot with Alex in the way. All around them the fighting was beginning to die down. The hired mercenaries were all dead and the few remaining Reapers were running away as fast as they could. The cabin was emptying, leaving only the three of them and a few of the Lions left. Alex was crushed under Nate's left arm. She could barely breath as he forced her to stand up straight. Jason continued to hold his gun pointed at Nate's head. There was nothing any of them could do.

Alex widened her eyes and motioned down towards her right with them. Jason saw the look and quickly shook his head, he knew what she was thinking and it was too risky. Alex tilted her eyes down again receiving another head shaking from Jason. Alex's left hand was free. She lifted it so that her balled up fist was laying against her stomach. She held her fist like that for a couple of seconds and then she flashed three of her fingers at Jason. He shook his head again. Her hand showed only two fingers. Jason readied his gun, begging her not to do this with his eyes. Only one finger remained.

One second later Alex dropped her last finger and a shot rang out.

Chapter 17

Nate fell as the bullet slammed into his head. The second Alex dropped her final finger she dove down to the right out of Nate's grasp and out of the way so Jason could make the shot. She fell down onto the floor beside Nate and lay there on her back. Jason ran to her side to help her up.

"Just give me a sec, Jason," she needed a chance to catch her breath. Her body ached despite the adrenaline coursing through her veins. She lifted her arms and put her hands over her face. The movement caused pain to shoot through her stomach and sides. She couldn't take a deep breath. Jason lifted her by both of her arms, the pain almost unbearable as she was placed on her feet. She leaned her body onto him and pressed her forehead against his. "You were trying to tell me something earlier?"

"I love you, Alex."

She leaned up and kissed him, "I love you, Jason." She paused and looked around amongst their friends. Some looked injured, but all were alive;

somehow although outnumbered, they had all made it. But one face was missing, "Where's Uncle Ronnie?"

Realization hit Jason: he hadn't seen his father since the fighting began. He let go of Alex and ran out the front door of the cabin to where his father was before the fighting began. Outside the cabin Leo and Kip were kneeling over a man lying on the ground pressing their hands into a wound on his stomach to try to stop the bleeding. Wade had managed to shoot Ron in the stomach before he ran into the cabin. Ron fought through the pain of the bullet, but had finally collapsed from loss of blood. Alex followed Jason outside and took in the sight before her. She ran to Ron's side with Jason, each of them taking one of his hands. He was still alive.

Ron looked at his son, "Jason."

"I'm right here, Dad."

"I love you." He turned his attention over to Alex, "Wade?"

"Dead."

Ron closed his eyes and nodded, "Alex, you're

father would've been proud of you."

"Was it true what Wade said about my mother?" Ron nodded again, his strength fading, "Why didn't you tell me?" Alex asked choking down a sob.

"I'm so sorry, Alex, about everything. I should have told you, but you were so young and you weren't ready. I'm sorry that I didn't do more for you."

"What are you talking about? You have been the best father and uncle that I've had. You've taken care of me and Jess our whole lives. I wouldn't be anywhere without you."

Ron shook his head, "I promised your father and your uncle that I would do whatever it took to make you a part of our club. You were supposed to become President when you were ready, you've been ready for a long time and I've selfishly kept you away. I didn't think you could handle it and I see now that I was wrong."

"What are you saying, Uncle? Last week you were barely ready to let me into the club. Now you're saying that I'm should be the President?"

"You're ready, even if you don't know it yourself. Please forgive me Alex."

Alex couldn't stop the tears from flowing now. She wrapped both of her hands around his and kissed the top of his hand, "There is nothing to forgive."

"I have always loved you and your sister like you were my own."

"We are your own."

"I am so proud of you like I know your father and mother would be." Ron turned his attentions back to Jason. "Alex will need a lot of help, she'll need you by her side. Serve as her Vice President as well as you have served me. Promise me that you will do for her what I have not done. Take care of Alex and Jesse and your mother. Your mother is going to have a hard time with this and she'll need you as well."

"I promise you I will. I will take care of them all. I love you, Dad."

"I love you too. Tell your mother and Jesse that I love them. I am proud of you both." Ron raised Alex and Jason's hands which were still clutching his and put them together. He let his hands fall back down to his sides leaving Alex and Jason's hands clasped together in front of him. That is how Ron died, joining his son and the girl whom he'd always loved as his daughter, together.

Chapter 18

Victor and Ryan pulled into the cabin's driveway shortly after the fighting had ended. Victor pulled the car over to the side and followed his partner to the place where Ron lay still on the ground. Jason and Alex were kneeling on either side of his body, crying. The rest of the Fu Lions were gathered around them, some of them also shedding tears.

The area was a disaster. There were bodies strewn across the front lawn and throughout the cabin. Bullet casings and bullets were scattered everywhere, making it impossible to walk without stepping on them.

Victor spoke up to the group, "You need to get out of here now."

Alex sat up, "We can't just leave him."

"I have to find a way to cover this mess up, Alex, and I can't do that if you're all still here. You have to go. I promise you that we will clean this mess up as quickly as possible."

Bobbie motioned for the others to leave.

Dennis, Kip, and Leo led the rest of the Lions back to their motorcycles to leave. Bobbie placed a hand on Jason's shoulder, "It's time to go, Jason. Everything will be alright, but we need to leave now."

Jason couldn't hold back his tears, "I can't."

"We have to."

Alex looked to Jason, then Sean who was standing beside her, and finally to Bobbie. "Bobbie is right, Jason. We have to go. Sean can you help me up?" Sean placed both of his hands under her arms and pulled her up off the ground. She took a sharp intake of breath that wracked her entire body with pain. She wiped the tears from her face walked around Ron's body towards the bikes. She offered Jason her hand as she walked by and he took it. Looking back only once, Jason followed Alex, Sean, and Bobbie to his motorcycle and together they left the cabin behind.

They rode the motorcycles straight to the clubhouse and met up with the others that had left before them. The members' families were in the bar waiting for the Lions' return. Jesse ran out front when she heard Jason and Alex pull into the parking lot. She waited for her sister to slowly unwind her arms from around Jason's waist and step down from the bike. Alex looked tired and in pain and the shirt she was wearing was covered in blood, but she was alive. Jesse fell into her sister's arms.

Sara waited in the doorway for Jason to approach. Some of the others had filed out into the parking lot behind Jesse and were watching when Jason walked up to his mother and told her that her husband would not be coming home. He didn't need to say the words, Sara knew by the looks on the faces of the other members, by the way that no one would say anything to her, but it was more than that; Sara could sense it. Sara crumpled. She put her hands over her face and leaned into her son's chest, her body wracked with sobs.

Wendy came running from the doorway and flung herself into Sean's arms before he could even get off his motorcycle. She sat in front of him on the bike with her legs wrapped around his torso as she kissed every inch of his face. The parking lot was filled with people greeting their loved ones: kisses, hugs, and tears were what the Lions found when they came home.

The Fu Lions members gathered in the meeting room to take a head count. They had to be sure that they hadn't lost anyone else amidst the confusion at the cabin. They entered the room and took their seats around the meeting table. There was only one empty chair.

The members moved back into the main bar room in the clubhouse and sat in silence as they waited to hear from Victor. They didn't drink, they didn't talk, they quietly sat around tables and on stools at the bar, unsure of what to do next. Alex was sitting on a stool between Jesse and Jason. Jesse clung to her sister not wanting to let her go. Sara remained sobbing in Jason's arms as she sat on the stool next to him. The phone rang, breaking the silence. The club members looked up from their seats to Jason and Alex expecting one of them to answer the call.

"Go ahead Jason," Alex told him. Jason let go of his mother and walked around the bar to answer the phone.

"This is Jason," he answered. The rest of them waited as Jason listened to the person on the other end of the line. The phone call only lasted about five minutes and then Jason said an abrupt "Thank you," and hung up the phone.

"That was Vic," he said to the curious faces staring at him. "He said that everything has been taken care of, we don't need to worry. The club is safe. Dad's body has been brought to the funeral home and we can go down there as soon as we're ready."

The forlorn group remained silent contemplating their next step. As Vice President of the club, Jason was expected to take the lead until the next vote when the club would choose a new President for the club. There were several things that the club would need to do over the next few days.

"What now?" Sean asked. The other

members turned their attention back to Jason, looking to him to lead.

"Now...now we need to have a vote. My father left something on the table as he died today."

"What was it?" Sean asked naively.

"He means that Ron made a suggestion that we need to discuss," Bobbie interjected.

"Oh, you mean Alex," Sean said.

"You all were there as my father said his last words. He died telling Alex that she was the rightful President of the club. In essence, he has put her name up for consideration despite the fact that she is not even a member of the Lions." Alex listened carefully to each word Jason was saying. He was standing in front of her facing the other members. This is not how things were normally done. They were in the main bar area out in the open instead of in the club's meeting room, and on top of that the members' families were all present. Never in the history of the club had things been done this way.

Jason continued, "I don't care what my father said. I am the Vice President of this club and it is my duty to take on the role as President until we vote. I have served this club loyally as a member for many years and even before that as I went through my trials to become a member. I deserve to be voted as our next President and as acting President it is my responsibility and right to nominate my opponent."

Alex's heart sunk from her chest, down into her stomach. She knew how Jason felt about her being a member and knew that he would never vote her in, let alone make her the next President of the Fu Lions. She knew that they would have to have a discussion about what Ron had told them before he died, but she didn't expect that it would happen this way or this soon. She looked up at Jason's back and watched as he turned to face her, his face unreadable.

"I nominate....Alex."

"What?!" Alex gasped as soon as the words were out of Jason's mouth.

"Alex, I was wrong before. I wanted to protect you because I love you, but I realize now that it was the wrong thing to do. You were always meant to be a part of our world...a part of this club. You were born to lead us. Your father and uncle knew that and so did my father. It's time for you to join us Alex. It's time for you to lead us."

Alex was speechless, she hadn't expected Jason to say these things and she didn't know how to respond. She dreamed of this moment her whole life, but now that her dream was so close in front of her she didn't know how to reach out and take it. She opened her mouth to say something, but no words came out. She sat on her stool and waited for him to say more, but he was finished. She looked over the faces in the rest of the room. Wendy, Sara, and most of the other women were completely shocked to be witnesses to the nomination. This was the first time in the history of the club that anything like this had ever happened. Alex needed to say something, but still no words came to her.

"I'll second that." It was Bobbie who stepped in to save her. "I second the nomination of Alex as our next President."

Jason nodded a "thank you" to Bobbie, "It's time to vote. Everyone in favor of Alex becoming our next President, please stand up."

Bobbie stood up from his chair at one of the tables. Because this was a vote for President Alex only needed the majority number of votes and not a unanimous one. The other members remained in their seats making their decision.

"I..." Alex started as the words finally came to her. "When I was a little girl I asked my father why there were no women in the club. His answer was that there had never been a woman who attempted to try and become a member. I asked him if there was a woman that wanted to become a member if the club would vote her in. He believed that one day it would be necessary for a woman to join the Lions and perhaps even lead them. Silly as I was as a little girl I asked him if there was a chance that I could be that woman and I'll never forget his answer as he kissed me goodnight. My father tucked me into bed and while he thought I was sleeping he whispered over me and said, 'I think that you'll grow up to be the only woman strong enough to lead the Lions.' I don't know if he was right, but I do know that I have spent my entire life working to earn your votes to become a member. I never asked to be the President or to lead you, but I believe that I can and I am begging you to give me a chance. I promise you that I will do everything I can to earn your respect and trust as your leader."

Alex stood next to Jason in front of the group as she gave them her speech. When she was finished Jason smiled at her and offered her his hand, which she grasped and squeezed as hard as she could. Together they stood, a united front, and awaited the group's decision.

"You've always had my respect and trust, and you've always had my vote." Leo stood up from his chair and gave Alex a little wink.

"You're the reason I got voted in the first place," Sean said as he stood, "and this time I can actually vote. I vote for Alex as our next President."

Five of the other members quickly followed after Sean, joining Bobbie and Leo. Alex had 8 votes out of 25, she only needed five more to have the majority.

Dennis stood from his seat and stared Alex in the face, "Alex, you've earned my vote," he said. Alex let out a breath that she hadn't realized she'd been holding in. She never foresaw what would happen next. Every chair in the room shifted as the rest of the members stood.

All 25 members of the Fu Lions were standing and alongside them their wives and children joined them. Alex Murphy was the President of the Fu Lions Motorcycle Club.

Sean kissed Wendy on the cheek and let her hand go when he realized that Alex had won the vote. He rushed out of the bar room and ran to "Murphy Automotive" across the parking lot. Everyone began to murmur to each other, wondering where could be going in a moment like this. Alex looked over Jason's shoulder and made eye contact with Wendy who shrugged her shoulders indicating she knew nothing about what Sean was doing. Leo winked at Jason who responded with a quizzical look.

When Sean returned he was pushing a

motorcycle beside him. He struggled to open the front door and hold the bike until Leo went over to assist him.

"Thanks Leo," Sean pulled the kickstand down with his foot, propping the bike up in the middle of the room for everyone to see. He smiled at Alex as he said, "Alex this is for you."

"Me?" Alex approached the motorcycle and ran her hands over the handlebars and down the bike until they stopped on the seat, inspecting it the whole way down. Her head snapped up, "Is this...? Really?"

"Yup. It's your father's bike. Ron brought it over about a week ago and asked me and Leo to get it set up for you. He said he knew you were going to need it really soon."

"He asked you to fix it up for me?" She turned and faced Jason who was now standing behind her next to the motorcycle, "He was planning this the whole time."

Chapter 19

Ron's funeral was held three days after the Lions voted Alex as their next President, on the day of the Cabin Battle as they now called it. The club held Ron's wake in the clubhouse were they placed his open coffin in their meeting room. The Lions, friends, family, and people from the town all took their turns filing into the meeting room to pay their last respects. Everyone present congregated in the bar where each one shared funny stories and experiences that they'd had with Ron. Ron was a good man and was going to be missed.

The Lions helped place Ron's closed coffin into the back of the hearse rented from the local funeral home. They followed the hearse on their motorcycles as the families and some friends followed in their cars until they reached the town's small cemetery. Ron was taken to the burial plot owned by the Fu Lions where he was buried amongst the other members long past. His was buried beside Jim Murphy, Alex's real uncle and one of Ron's closest friends.

Ron was slowly lowered into the ground, into his final resting place. Sara wept beside the grave as she held her son's hand. When Ron was gently placed into the ground Sara bent over taking a handful of dirt and threw it into the hole on the top of his coffin. Jason bent down beside her and did the same. He helped his mother up off the ground and watched as Alex and Jesse threw their dirt into the grave. The rest of the funeral party followed their example.

Alex didn't stay at the grave to watch as the rest of the club said their final goodbyes. Instead she left her sister and walked over to the place where her father was buried. He was buried only two spaces to the left of Ron, but no one was paying attention to this section of the cemetery plot as she knelt down and rubbed her hand across her father's name on his headstone. The headstone read:

Kevin Murphy, Jr.
Beloved Father, Brother, Husband and Friend.
He will be Sorely Missed.

"Sorely missed is right," Alex whispered to her father. "I did it, Dad." She remained kneeling next to her father's grave until she heard someone's footsteps approaching from behind.

"It's time," Jason said. Alex smiled to herself and took Jason's offered hand to help her up. She was still sore from the Cabin Battle where she had received three broken ribs. Jason kissed her, "Ready?"

"Yes." They walked hand in hand to their motorcycles. The Lions had a tradition: after each President was voted into their position, the new President would then lead the Lions in a motorcycle ride through the main street of town and around the territory that they had just sworn to protect. The Lions had postponed their ride until Ron's body was buried for the sake of Jason and Sara, but now it was time for Alex to take her rightful place and to lead the Lions.

Jesse approached Alex on her motorcycle before she could pull away. Alex smiled weakly at her younger sister. She reached into her pocket and took out their father's pocket knife.

"I want you to have this, Jess. It was Dad's favorite knife. I've kept it with me every day since he died and it's saved my life twice over the past few weeks. I think it's time for you to have it." She placed the knife in Jesse's open palm and closed her fingers around it. "You're ready." She hugged her little sister and finished strapping her helmet on.

Alex looked behind her and saw that the rest of the Lions were waiting for her to lead the way. She started her father's motorcycle, now custom fit to her, and revved the engine.

The engines roared like Lions as they pounded through the main street of town. Traffic had been cleared and redirected to make room for the motorcycles. The people of the town stood on their front lawns, in grocery store parking lots, and on the sidewalks as they watched their protectors' ride by. Alex and Jason led the way side by side, the way they planned to remain for the rest of their lives as all 25 Lions followed behind them.

The Fu Lions. Regal beasts from ancient Chinese folklore believed to have mythical powers that were used to protect people from evil spirits. Two stone lions would be placed outside palaces and other important buildings in order to protect the people within. We may not have magical powers like these lions, but we have assumed their role. We fight to protect the people within our town from the many evils that try to push themselves in. We will not allow our town to be used as a center for selling drugs or illegal weapons. We will not allow our people to be threatened or abused or to succumb to the power of drugs. The Reaper's Sons are finished for now, but one day they will come back. They will regroup themselves and come back even stronger than they were before and when they get here we will be waiting for them. This time we will be ready and we will finally take them down once and for all.

I never asked to be a leader of men, but it is what I have become. My father always knew that I would. There are two stone lions standing at the entrance to our clubhouse: one male and one female, the way it should be, the way my great-grandfather knew it would be. They are a pair and can only be complete and able to protect when they are together. The club has been through hard times--they were incomplete--but now I am here and they are whole. Together we can protect our town from anything. I swore to my Uncle Jimmy on his deathbed that I would protect the club and protect our town. This is my birthright, my responsibility, my duty. This is my club. This is my town.

Epilogue

Darkness filled the sky and crept along the ground slowly until it covered the surface of the world like a blanket. The log cabin sat alone and abandoned in the dark looming woods. The bodies of fallen men were scattered on the ground left where they fell, waiting to be claimed and collected. Bronze bullet shells covered the ground and cabin floors. Nothing moved, nothing breathed, not a single sound was made.

A gasp, a sharp intake of breath from lungs that had previously stopped taking in air, a man sat up abruptly from where he was lying on the floor. He was confused. It took several minutes for him to remember where he was. He took off his black shirt and removed the bulletproof vest he had been wearing underneath. There were three bright red marks on his stomach from where the bullets hit the vest. The marks were already changing color from red to a light blue and purple. He was badly bruised and it hurt to breathe. The vest saved his life and he was thankful he had been smart enough to put it on, his men had not been so smart.

The man took his time standing up from the floor. There was a deep gash on the side of his right leg that was bleeding badly. He undid his belt from his waist and made it into a tourniquet for his leg, securing it tightly to his upper thigh. He slowly hobbled out of the back room and into the main room in the cabin. He checked the bodies of his dead men not looking for survivors, but for a weapon. He found a gun with a full magazine lying next to one of the bodies on the floor. The man moved farther into the room, stepping over another body.

A hand gripped his leg. The man stopped and looked down at the body on the floor. The man on the floor was still alive despite a scary wound on his cheek.

"Help me," Nate said. Jason's bullet went through Nate's cheek and out the lower back of his neck. The injury made him pass out, but it did not kill him. "Take me with you," he repeated and let go of the man's leg.

"Help you?" The man nodded, "Ok, I'll help you. I made you a deal earlier, didn't I? Fail me again and I'll kill you," he paused and then shrugged. "Well a deal's a deal."

Wade cocked his gun and fired. Nate's raspy breathing stopped and his head slumped back down on the floor. Wade looked around the cabin. He had wasted his money on the mercenaries who were now all dead, and he had lost most of his men. The Murphy girl had gotten the better of him but he would not allow it to stay that way.

There was nothing left for him here in this town, he would have to leave and start again before he could get his revenge on Alex Murphy. He left the cabin and headed for the cover of the woods. First he would find what was left of his men and they would re-group, then they would start again. He would rebuild everything the Lions had taken from him and he would be back.

<u>About the Author</u>

Alyssa Rae is a creative writer and piano teacher who was born in New England. She currently resides in a small historic town in North Carolina. This is her debut novel. She has several works in progress, stay tuned...

Visit the author's website at www.alyssarae.com

.

www.ingramcontent.com/pod-product-compliance
Lightning Source LLC
Chambersburg PA
CBHW062016170626
46813CB00001B/184